The Marble Corridor

Ryan Madej

The Marble Corridor

Ryan Madej

JEF Books/Depth Charge Publishing
Aurora, Illinois

Published as JEF 87

ISBN 1-884097-87-1
ISBN-13 978-1-884097-87- 4
ISSN 1084-847X

Offbeat / Quirky Books
JEF Books/Depth Charge Publishing
"The Foremost in Innovative Publishing"
experimentalfiction.com

JEF Books are distributed to the book trade by SPD: Small Press Distribution and to the academic journal market by EBSCO

Dedication

To the memory of my friend and fellow writer, Will Bernardara, an uncompromising, rebellious soul. Rest easy.

"There are no people in what I've written. Only ghosts."

Susan Sontag

THE MARBLE CORRIDOR
a book of fragments

The 52nd Degree

I'll begin by saying this: everything written on these pages is basically true, yet at the same time treading the line between two distinct worlds which I've only glimpsed. Up to this point, through the chaos that is time, memory, and fantasy, I've been able— without fear or need of censure— to describe what I've seen, and hopefully what I have gained from these experiences. To be clear, this is not an autobiography or memoir, but rather an attempt to outline the fringes of consciousness. Like any story there are characters, and perhaps two of the most important are Jorge Luis Borges and Franz Kafka. The two writers whose shadows still linger on the walls of literature, continually haunting me with every pen stroke. I might even go so far to say that they are the bricks and cement for the distorted tower I've created in my mind...

Five of Borges's stories I go back to frequently, but one— barely two pages— I've read countless times, maybe even emulating it on some level ever since. The story is *Covered Mirrors* from his short story collection *The Maker,* and without saying much else it involves the coming together of masculine and feminine forces in a rather strange, awkward way. The feeling of this story lead me elsewhere over the years toward someone in-between Kafka and Borges: Ryūnosuke Akutagawa, who, incidentally Borges admired. The same could be said of the Argentinian's love of Kafka when he penned that superb essay *Kafka and his Precursors.*

Maybe, just maybe, each was a reflection of the other...Three points in a Triangle...Symbolizing not only literary greatness, but a trinity of mystery.

As I walked through the decrepit backstreets in the Western Quarter, a heavy drift of old memories slid across the edge of my mind. Impressions and images from a dense period of my life... What happened then? Can I even remember the time and place? A melody of unseen notes and subtle music behind the curtains or in a wisp of smoke. Something was there, waiting.

I passed by a storefront of paraffin wax masks of women whose features seemed to resemble the faces of women I knew, or perhaps even *would know in the future*. Each had a distinct colour to them, and as I looked past the masks I could see what appeared to be the owner, sitting in a large, plush armchair, smoking a pipe.

He smiled widely and I kept on walking.

*

A rumour persisted in the city about a ghost train that ran through the river valley. Many people swore to its existence and attested to hearing the clanging bells as it weaved its way across the High Gate Bridge. The bridge entrance, which opens onto a foot path nearly a kilometre long, looked reminiscent of the Rashomon with the same peeling red lacquer. Many times I crossed the bridge at night with its dim luminescence above me and a sense of dread below me as I looked into the murky waters. An old saying about the nature of the river, the Velox: *Never pass by the river at twilight. You, weary traveller, are liable to fall in due to the tricks of the*

water spirit that inhabits its waters." I came to realize
in the midst of wide-open space that there is no
prescription strong enough to dull the sensation of
impending death. Actually, on the contrary, that's not
true: the embracing of mystery tends to be the soothing
balm the further I dive into myself...Maybe this
occurred for the simple reason we endlessly drift
everyday toward the ultimate mystery on a distant
shore...Of course, this is all hearsay.

*

They silently bloom as all other flowers do, but their
fragrance induces a deep sleep producing terrible
nightmares. A. imbued these flowers with a rich texture
of shadow, leading me to believe that behind all beauty
lies a smattering of darkness. She came here in the way
they all did, on a train from the Outskirts through the
only entrance and exit, the Marble Corridor. Her
essence— or rather the blueprint of her life source—
stood between the claws of the Crab and the vestal
Virgin. Her brightness, like the Sun, was only a
disguise. I began asking myself if she might have been
a regular visitor to the man with the masks— sitting as

a model for the multiple personalities that he hung in his window.

We walked across the High Gate Bridge once, at the turn of the New Year, in the very dead of an unseasonably warm winter night. She said: *When I was a girl, I could see the edge of darkness coming over the horizon, slowly but surely in my direction waiting to consume me. That seemed so long ago, eons in my mind, but I didn't know what it was that spurred me to embrace it gently and accept the power it radiated.* Me in response: *And what was it? Something tangible?* She said: *About as tangible as a shadow— visible but ever present beside you. I felt it in the midst of that beautiful place, full of exotic flowers and butterflies.* Me: What place was that? She looked at me with serious eyes and said: *Paradise, of course.*

*

The summer— 95?— is when the universe conspired to shake my spirit. If it was the summer of 1995, I would have been 16 years old and visiting my sister in the Eastern Flatlands. During a trip to a second hand bookstore, I perused the shelves holding out little hope of finding anything worth reading as my fingers caressed the spines of old romance novels, cookbooks, and thrillers. To my amazement Orwell's *1984* lay wedged between a series of forgettable titles, and a little further on is where I first laid eyes on Kafka's *The Trial.* A strange twist of fate.

In retrospect— through the hallucinatory lens called time— one has no idea how a work of art will transform thoughts, actions or spirit, but it would seem the most sincere works always will. Both books proved to be the antidote to a sickness I didn't know I had, a disease called boredom. My reading habits permanently changed after absorbing those defining works. What surprised me years later is how similar a feeling they conveyed despite their obvious differences...The world as prison and labyrinth; the world as faceless and tortuous; the world as mysterious and ultimately unknowable.

The shadows of those two novels still hangs over my heart like heavy talismans, each holding a power like no other. And yes, that shadow looms large, for there are moments in the early morning hours still under the haze of sleep when I wonder if a pair of men in black will come to my door to take me away. During those times I shut my eyes, hoping the gentleness of sleep will find me again.

*

When I walk past shuttered windows, down darkened halls, empty passages, or lonely roads, I get closer to that elusive goal that I know nothing about other than it's somewhere that I must reach. Eyes sore and red due to lack of sleep under a roof of continuous sickness. Morning beckons. Every day is a chance to begin again and reset the cosmic clock and watch the sun spill surreptitiously over the horizon. Dreams are lost and only a few razor-sharp shards remain on the precipice; a precipice that looks down into a warm, inviting abyss that inevitably snakes back into the heart of the city where I was born.

I think I've left, but really, I've gone nowhere.

*

The sheer lack of light became the stimulant that eventually became the narcotic, the addiction by which I measured myself. Darkness, *true darkness*, became every bit as interesting and seductive as anything tangible. And just like tangible addictions, the results were nearly fatal. I entered the Corridor so long ago that my initial memory of its landscape I can barely remember. The dim fluorescence of the train platform at night with its handful of travellers high or drunk, quiet or bursting with prophetic verse still makes my body stiffen and my thoughts turn cold. Only the smell of the spring rainfall dancing over the city streets and that intense ozone scent reaching my nostrils give me pause here in the Land of the Dead.

As Banville put it in his novel *Ghosts:* "*My horizon had been limited for so long, high walls make the gaze turn inward.*" I thought about those words as I stared off into the distance from my old balcony north of Salamander Road, not far from the empty skyline where the original train line used to run. As a young boy the area almost resembled prairie, and the openness that stretched from east to west would give way to the deathly hooves of the Iron Horse. Casting my eyes west, I would think of our old house nestled in the pre-war streets, and how during that time of conflict in our history that used to be the edge of the city. One has to wonder what it all looked like before...Before the movement of the wheel and the laying of brick. We tread on the graveyards of the shamans, warriors, and animals now— walking hand in hand with spectres.

*

A cigarette at the Gothic Arch (After Piranesi). The lay of the land in the midst of steam and fog is really just a blur of half-formed images, and the four districts dedicated to the Four Founders are four quarters and four elemental sources. Agni (Interzone), Isis (Rubicon), Vayu (The Istanbul), and The Rainbird (Trinacrium). The scene in my head: nightfall in the summer near the arcade, my bike propped up against the wall, kids puffing dope, knowing there would be no light on at home when I arrived. The key that would let me in the house only served to keep me from the unknown of the growing darkness, talking me away from the rivers of soma flowing outside my window. Inert and still, time unmoving, eyes seeking light and unveiling the secret within me. I would often look in the mirror and mimic people and accents to keep myself occupied as I waited for my Father. Waiting in silence always proved to be difficult. Hours passing that had no true feeling or description, only a dense, empty presence. The television didn't work properly and the phone line had been cut off due to non-payment. I would sometimes shuffle to the bathroom, running the water until it was warm and splash some over my face...eyes puffy and red...my feet sore from too much walking. After a while I would just go to bed, sit on the edge and turn toward the window, forgetting there was nothing for me to see.

*

The Guidebook Maker

Around 1844, the famous guidebook maker Karl Baedeker had this to say about the city of Midtown in its infancy: *"Midtown is quiet and subdued, yet it has the ambition and drive inherent of any city caught in a unique time and space with a flair for the ancient in its architecture and general design. One can also tell as they walk the streets— in particular the Dragon Court— that calamity could greet the tourist or idle flaneur at any moment. I would say Midtown has a resemblance to cities such as Paris or Rome, though it's more fitting to say the image of this city on the plains is closer in spirit to places I've not yet glimpsed but only heard about. Cities like Raissa, Marozia, and Theodora...*

*

Beckett

In the world of Molloy, Malone, and all the others is a world— a familiar world. The world turns more expansive the further you go, but at the same time disintegrating into dust. No one wrote better minimal prose than Beckett. I've never read *Waiting for Godot, Endgame, or Krapp's Last Tape,* as they are plays and need to be seen. The only exception I make to reading plays is Shakespeare, and as we know the Bard is immortal in this regard. Beckett, on the other hand, is immortal to me as well, albeit in a different way that can't be accurately described on paper. Beckett is more of a mindset, a way of thinking about the world through the miniscule, the repetitive, the tragicomic, and the circumference of the unknown. He is Joyce's counterpart: the troubadour of emptiness.

My first encounters with Beckett were through the story of Joyce and *Finnegans Wake*— a book that will remain unread for centuries and be discovered by a future culture as some sort of literary Rosetta Stone. Anyway, Beckett came into my life as I was absorbing a year's worth of geography in order to graduate high school, and I recall reading the *Texts for Nothing* after dropping off some modules downtown for grading. My anxiety had been climbing as I was going to make graduation by the skin of my teeth. Too much extracurricular reading and not enough studying. Reading Beckett was no exception: literature had almost trumped everything else in my life when it came to educating myself, which in time would become a bigger problem.

Yet as I read the *Texts for Nothing*— in particular number six, which will always be my favorite part of Beckett— I started to see the desolation of the modern world for the first time. Not in the same bleak way Sartre saw it, or how Camus saw it through his character Meursault, but the lens of bare consciousness and the landscape it created. These solitary beings traversing empty lands and impossible dimensions of space looking for a way out, but finding little to satisfy them.

The only motivation was to keep going. So yes, I've kept on going in spite of myself; in spite of great failures and small triumphs; in spite of the unknown and the all too familiar; in spite of everything, really. Isn't that all of us? Or at least most of us? We, those disembodied voices in the Void screaming out, hoping to be heard? Like the

Unnamable of Beckett's trilogy— armless and legless—
we carry on. That is what Beckett has taught me: to
carry on despite myself.

*

A Short History of Fire

...His life ended (?) sometime before the advent of the
master Fulcanelli, who wrote what is considered the
final genuine books on transmutation. Bastion Perrot
had a vision of a man who could manipulate fire with
his mind and could not be singed by the flames. Taking
the visions as a good omen, he began preparations for the
ceremony of the White Salamander on which his fame
rests.

"*Whiten the flame and burn your books*" was the credo
he lived by and often told his acolytes— words he said
must be remembered if one was to attain true spiritual
cleansing. He also said, as documented in his later
journals, "*When spring arrives with its promises of
renewal and possibility, remember too the rose that
heats the spirit and molds the spirit.*"

Many decades later at 59 Rue Rochechouart the operations of the fires made Fulcanelli the stuff of legend, and like any true master, he too, vanished.

*

The Primal Fire

Late at night I may need to call him in the future: the Ram. He would meet me in an open field with a shovel in one hand and a joint in the other. The pale light of the moon would reflect off his dark skin and all he would say is "*What's going on, bro?*" He would then pass the joint to me in a calm fashion and glance over my shoulder..."*What's in the trunk?*" I say nothing. The pull of the full moon and the pull I take from the joint leaves me speechless but ready to listen. Off in the distance I hear him open the trunk and under his breath whisper: "*What the fuck did you do, guy?*"

Coming back to reality, but still lost in abstract thought, I wander over to the trunk and stare wordlessly at the corpse. Looking at me with acute seriousness he says: "*We need to get to work.*" He says he never thought he would get a call like this, but a promise is a promise, after all. That's what I like about him: reliability, loyalty. Two key things sadly missing today in most people.

Secrets are safe with him, and his with me— a bond, a deep bond beyond normal understanding, or in this case circumstance. We dig for what seems like days and he doesn't crack a sweat. The air is cool and refreshing and for the first time since I arrived I feel a bit relaxed. We dig some more until we know the hole is deep enough. I remember when I first met him well over fifteen years ago, and how all those late nights translated into what was occurring now on the darkest of nights; the dark night of the soul, lit by the moon. We smoked a lot then, played chess, threw darts, oblivious to the possibility of being in our current situation, yet totally ready for it at any moment.

We toss the corpse into the hole and push the dirt in, taking our time, sharing a quick laugh then lighting another joint as the wind changes. So, what now? I say, almost inaudibly. He looks to the sky saying nothing, which really says everything. We drive off in opposite directions and never speak of this again. A true bond...

*

Pale Fire

The desire to paint oneself as another is always a tempting activity to indulge in, but so few of us gather enough courage to do so. John Shade was one of those people who was unafraid of the consequences...or was he? The only person we can ask, or at least examine, is Charles Kinbote, a biographer of sorts who set out to tell us who John Shade really was as a person. Instead, we seem to learn more about Kinbote himself and the strange and winding roads he takes one his own journey. One can't help but notice that the 999-line poem he sets out to interpret— apparently written by Shade— seems like the reflections of a man in peril. Who better than the noble Kinbote to comment on such a piece of work? The duplicity that evolves out of this masterfully wrought story is analogous to life, isn't it? I often found myself asking the question as I was reading who and what I was, or continue to be, as the years disappear. The answer: ?

*

Rubicon/The Isis Plaza

"It is not just these games I have thought up— I have also thought up a great deal about the house. Each part of the house occurs many times; any particular place is another place."

The House of Asterion

For the greater part of two years (longer, perhaps?) the world as I saw it appeared opaque and impenetrable, in much the same way Kafka's works can often be impenetrable. You can often see the shape or dimensions but not know its depths until you find a crack to slip through. I've seen Midtown as a mass of malevolent force that has stayed with me all these years despite attaining a sounder mind and body. In much the same way Kafka is synonymous and a *part of* Prague, in a literal and literary sense, so too Midtown is synonymous with me. When all is said and done, the picture that I'm left with is more dream than reality.

Never would I see the city I was born into as the same place that I'll eventually die in. That place no longer exists to me, even as I walk its streets every day. People are ghosts as much as they are soft, malleable flesh in this familiar but alien place I call Home. A description would suffice even if it's only a sketch of what I perceived in places not yet found by my waking self.

*

Me and the Bull spent a lot of time in the Plaza throughout the early years when days were infinite gems set upon the good frame that was Salamander Road. Our conversations long forgotten, I can only speculate on what we might talk about now in the din of a lost era, hearing the voices echoing across miles of sprawl, giving way to feverish coupling and wet kisses in the underground bars where the relay cameras capture it all imperfect colour.

During the summer months, the dying light over the horizon turned the plaza a deep blue as we left the video arcade or the bookstore, signifying a changing of the guard. I might have said: "*Twilight is a dangerous time you know. Ancient people likened this part of the day to the appearance of bad spirits and the like.*" He might have responded: "*So you believe that then? Especially here?*" Me: "*Here more than anywhere.*" We might then look at the sky and the fiery glow fade surreptitiously over the horizon, parting ways as we wandered through tree-lined streets only to do it all over again tomorrow.

18-Moon-A Fool's Life (After Akutagawa)

"*Her face seemed bathed in a moonglow even now, in daylight. As he watched her walk on (they had never met), he felt a loneliness he had not known before,*"

(The Door)

The Door always swings inward. That is what I was told in the past, the distant past, by the Twins who asked me to pass over the Threshold. Those same Twins never returned, though their voices come to me through invisible means known as the Muted Horn, or Trystero. The entrance to the door is *always changing*. Keep that in mind if you're ever trying to find me.

(The Wall)

Once you walk a little further, you will inevitably hit a wall— a wall that is just high enough that you will not be able to reach the top. With that in mind, you may need to detour or find some way over the Wall itself, though I must say that that is not an easy task.

(The Twins)

Remember those twin girls in *The Shining* who frighten Danny as he pedals his way through the Overlook? The Twins were like them, only older of course, more shapely and beautiful, but equally as frightening in their respective ways in how they *communicated*. One, through the flesh...the other through the mouth. The two aspects never crossed over into one being, always distinct and fully aware of their singular power. The Flesh spoke thus: *Fuck me as though it is the solution to the problem you have. Do it with ease and forget how weak it makes you feel in the End. The only true happiness is to be wrapped in another person's skin.*

That whole period is a skittering blur, as it should be. No congruency or symmetry is left from that time. What was once perfect, sublime, and carnal is a smattering of dead feelings and impressions. Nights of dim lights coupled with moist kisses is all that remains, like all those memories from before.

The Other Twin will have to wait.

(Absence)

There are only the barest flickers of light once you take a wrong turn and end up where I am... (wherever that may be in the grand scheme) and sadly I've ended up somewhere amongst the bones and shattered glass of yesterday. The question is: "how did this happen?" Then I begin to think my mind has begun a slow disintegration into nothingness, because no *rational* person can have these ideas and actually believe them.

*

The Trystero

The Muted Horn is another name it's given. Actually, I gave it that name. But some of you have seen it before and might recognize its shape. The Trystero is a mouthpiece, a way of communicating; the eyes of the dead that can see through everything. Strangely I find myself closing my own eyes, slipping in and out of consciousness. When I open them, the night has spilled over me and the Trystero has led me once again over the Threshold of the Marble Corridor. I want to shatter that part of me that has come undone and feed it to the dogs. Nothing would give me more pleasure than erasing what I see as undesirable. If I look into the occasional window, I might see a shadow or two dancing on the walls, fondling one another in some two-dimensional coupling, merging into one. Then I listen. A voice says: *Kill what you don't understand.* Response: *So how do I kill the world, then?* The voice says: *You can't. You just keep on moving...*

*

Sebald

"Whenever a shift in our spiritual life occurs and fragments such as these surface, we believe we can remember. But in reality of course, memory fails us." WG Sebald, *The Rings of Saturn*

Journal Entry, dated July 12th 1997/ Our bodies are given life from the midst of nothingness.

The night breathes slowly as it passes over me. My mind and emotions are in their proper places and everything is illuminated. I've put a light blanket around myself while I sit here writing. I've come to realize that anything of worth in my life resides here in one form or another: pictures, writings, music, chessboard, books, etc. It's my one true sanctuary. My desk is where I feel the most comfortable these days, which allows me to look upon the dusty road outside my window or gaze at the stars on clear nights. I sip vermouth and gin, smoke Thai stick, breathe. In the Buddhist *Dhammapada,* the chapter on The World states the following: *One who looks upon the world as a bubble and a mirage, that person the King of Death cannot see...*

If only I had read that sooner, so I could have treated the world as a desert with so many illusory oases, rather than waste my time. What prevented me from leaving this city was my own fear; fear of opening the door to the outside world. So much of my dreaming leads back to the primal waters, seeing myself sitting at the foot of the mountains on the cusp of the ocean, where the movements of rivers and lakes lie at the stillest point, listening with my eyes closed to the currents with a desire to drown myself in them. After all, Camus said suicide is the only true philosophical question.

I mean, really, what else could it be?

The Many Faces of Fernando Pessoa

"*I'm liberated and lost. I feel. I shiver with fever. I'm I.*" The Book of Disquiet

José Saramago, author of many fine novels— most notably, *Blindness*—wrote a book called *The Year of the Death of Ricardo Reis.* An interesting title to say the least: mysterious, provocative, and an allusion of things to come. What proved to be the selling point for me, other than the fact I enjoyed Saramago's novels, was the name Ricardo Reis. I had heard the name mentioned somewhere before, and after some time thinking about it, I realized the name was one of the heteronyms of Fernando Pessoa, the famous poet of Lisbon. What makes the novel so interesting, at least from what I can recall, is that Ricardo Reis is frequently visited by the spectre of the deceased poet. So in essence the protagonist— a character who was fictional, but also the *reflection* of a real poet— was visited by the spirit of the dead poet is strange, but appropriate considering Pessoa himself.

I read *The Book of Disquiet* at a particularly disquieting time in my own life, filled with uneasy sleep, intense anxieties, and anti-depressant drugs. The book is a collection of philosophical musings from the pen of another Pessoa ghost, Bernardo Soares, who seemed to share many of the same afflictions I was suffering from. Pessoa himself was a loner and alcoholic, and at that point I could identify with the man and his creations.

As brilliant as *The Book of Disquiet* is, there are two instances in Pessoa's life that intrigue me more: the discovery of 25,000 pages of manuscript after his death and the fact that infamous occultist Aleister Crowley enlisted him to fake his own death, which didn't amount to much.

Pessoa created hundreds of these personas, each with their own personalities and foibles, perhaps as props in which to hide behind, for life was too cruel. This is what writing is essentially: a means to hide oneself amidst the expectations and facts...

*

The Midtown Book of the Dead

A warm, late summer breeze brushes over me. Rose petals cover a section of the concrete, which I find strange yet lovely. Is it still Sunday? I ask myself, then walk toward Salamander Road. After a block or two of cheerless scenes I head north toward the Old Library. Many of the buildings I pass are familiar run-down shops of all kinds: bookstores, antique dealers, purveyors of herbs and aphrodisiacs, terrible restaurants. Places I used to dwell, often alone, hoping I would come to some sort of epiphany or find some rare artifact that would open and reveal some great insight into nature.

Now I feel just as she said I would: like an unknown, a ghost, someone who barely existed at all. The streets are deserted and the dead calm rises up to meet me like a wave that never fully crests, but stays suspended around me, making me shiver a little despite the heat...

She was right about one thing at least.

*

Locks, Black Holes

-Every lock has a key. One can spend their whole life looking for the right key in the wrong places, the map gets wet, you're given wrong directions, or you figure out when it's too late that the way forward is the way back. Once you're at the start again, the skyline has changed immensely...

-Why are you telling me this? Just in a philosophical mood or what?

-I've been having these strange dreams.

-What kind of dreams?

-Dreams where I'm standing in a maze of concentric circles that slowly fill up with water. The water is not murky but very clear. Once, only once, in the many times I've dreamt this was I lifted from the pool by a woman whose face I couldn't see...She kissed me lightly then...

-What, then what?

-Nothing...then nothing...a black hole

I didn't push the conversation any further because I could see the distress in his face. He said he had to leave as it was getting late. He vanished not long after that night we spent talking, never to be seen again.

*

The 12th Degree

Deciphering the past is like trying to make sense of the Voynich manuscript. In other words, interpreting the symbols that appear. Sometimes the meanings are obvious, while other times— meaning most of the time— we find ourselves digging for answers.

VIII, IX, XI

Symbols are useless without some frame of reference, but it is far more useful to create your own. This much I learned from the Knights of the Eastern Calculus. I learned a similar lesson on the Lost Highway, a road that inevitably lead me back to where I started. Grey light fell on me heading back via train from the Waterfront Market. Empty car. The lights began to fail as we pulled into each station, but no one got on. Then laughter, then whispers, maybe a heartbeat dissolving and dissipating with the movement of the train.

A wise man (whose name is lost or forgotten, which really amounts to the same thing) said: *"Everything that begins as comedy, inevitably ends as mystery."* But had he lived a little longer he may have said: *"Everything that begins as mystery inevitably ends as mystery."*

Sometime after, between gazing at the stars and the clouds of acrid smoke, I roamed the Pavilion Arcade in the Dragon Court somewhat lost in thought about mirrors. My reflection appeared clouded, as though there was a slight haze in the glass which seemed on the verge of cracking. I said to myself in a soft, almost elegiac tone: *"I want to shatter that part of myself that has come undone and feed it to the dogs. Nothing would give me more pleasure than erasing what I see as undesirable."*

No one around to listen...the paralysed force of winter reflected itself back to me in the glass. Blue, red, paper dreams lying between the why and when of how I got there. A sharpened knife in my hand and a gin bottle in the other. Hollow laughter...

And from all that I have two distinct visions of the Crab saving me, tolerating me, writing me letters. "*Why fear it? Why not embrace the communion shared with another not so unlike yourself? What about all that you'll gain? Make your own moments...Are you okay right now?*"

Oh, I'm okay, I told myself and made my own moments under a haze of smoke. The afternoon rain felt good upon my skin, and I realized many years later that Mantra Hand came into my life shortly thereafter, directing the following:

Letter One (I see you)

Hello dear. Twilight. Cold, inactive streets. I saw you sitting in the One Twelve eating cheap ramen and reading a dog-eared copy of Robbe-Grillet's *The Erasers*. You would be sure to let the police know of my whereabouts if this letter was ever to be read by your dark blue eyes. Yes, those eyes that stared off into the distance as you stood outside my door with your back against the wall. Eyes that would be equally fascinating under glass, in formaldehyde, or in a cupboard.

I see you. I see you by the Great Basilica. I see you by the bronze horse and that decrepit phone booth on Salamander Road. I see you sipping martinis in the Blue Hour Lounge or the Arcana. I see you walking across empty parking lots into the underground and out of sight.

Remember, you're never far from me.

*

Doors

...The room, which really couldn't be called a room at all, but a narrow elongated hallway that seemed to stretch out further than my eyes could see, reminded me of a story whose details were buried deep in my mind. Mirrors of various shapes and sizes, statues depicting animals frozen in various positions. Some of these animals were mystical in nature: *The Eight-Forked Serpent of Koshi, the Phoenix, and the Lunar Hare.*

A vision: Empty plains and railway tracks running outward past the walls, a murder of crows, a man in sunglasses counting keys on a ring, a tree bearing the hanged body of Judas. As I progressed down the hall the walls widened, leading me into a vast triangular epicentre reminiscent of a sacred tomb that may have been the resting place of a king, or a virgin queen. Why I thought this I cannot say for sure, my surroundings were tangible enigmas evoking old feelings, creating an unclear space in my mind like cities wrapped in fog...

*

Diaries (1)

The Colour of Sleep.

A pronounced desire to stop time and sleep for a year, stirring in the juices of unconscious landscapes. Thoughts of mountains and rivers. Perhaps the secret lies in the river, a river diverting itself into the Unknown. Always easier to return than to depart, for arrival summons the comfortable, the familiar, the tangible, whereas departure can summon up fear, loneliness, uncertainty, as much as it does excitement and desire. Departure then is a kind of sleep. When we travel we put the familiar and the mundane to bed, letting it slip away until we awake again in its arms.

Cities all carry secrets, untold stories, micro histories, shrouded in a past written in code— walled and cut-off from the outside world just like the deepest parts of ourselves.

The other cities were dead, or at least left to die after all was said and done, leaving masses of people to wander much like their ancestors over ice floes and mountain passes, across rivers and prairies, forests and waterfalls...All was not lost however, for out there lay an opportunity to begin again... a chance to find hidden gold.

The Eleventh of September, 2004
...My mind continues to shift in all directions, awakening me to a treasure trove of ideas. From good photography, death, revenge, beauty...I want to take a leave of absence from work for at least a month so I can organize my thoughts, my work, my life— another year is almost gone and I see things slipping away before me in a haze of fragments, deliriums, and empty words.

The Sixteenth of November, 2004
"*Danger, disquiet, anxiety attend the unknown.*"

The Eighteenth of June, 2005

I had a terrible night physically— drank too much gin far too fast. Vomited in my room. I was in a fearful state for half an hour before passing out.

The Twelfth of April, 2009

T.S. Eliot from *The Wasteland*. "*I read much of the night and go south in the winter.*" Nothing can ever be that simple. We live in a world made complicated by our desires.

*

"*The city seems to deliver itself at the onset... Kiosks, arc lamps, buildings crystallize into figures that are never to return.*" Walter Benjamin

A man waits to depart in the Marble Corridor terminus. The night heaves itself upon him as it used to heave itself upon me, but the difference is how I listen to falling rain and lean on the window sill to smell the open air infused with ozone. Days and moons past I would have lit a cigarette and just contemplated the destinations of the freights that moved through the city like heavy footed ghosts.

For years a dream pursued me. It still does from time to time. An empty, virtually light-less room with a bed, my limp nearly lifeless body upon it, waiting for death. The dream almost seemed like it came from another life led in another dimension. As the rain fell today these terrible yet strangely comforting thoughts came to me then receded like the tides...

*

Letter 2 (Face of Another)

The sweet-smelling air drifts in through my window...Or should I say *your* window. Your cat greeted me by rubbing up against my leg, still drawn somehow to my scent, which surprisingly is not musky and old smelling as you used to describe it during those long nights fuelled by alcohol and Lebanese Blond hash, as we sat close in the great space of your living room watching Teshigahara films over and over. I washed my face in the bathroom and made sure to touch familiar objects: hairpins, combs, toothbrush, even the slim bar of soap you use to lather your legs before shaving them...

Nothing is sacred. No one is sacred. Even you.

I looked in the mirror and I saw someone else entirely staring back.

See you soon.

*

Night Walking

"I cannot walk through the suburbs in the solitude of the night without thinking that the night pleases us because it suppresses idle details, just as our memory does." Borges.

The Lamplight Moth

It resembled a large piece of crystal, suspended over the street, glittering in the early morning din. But really it was not morning. I imagined it to be morning even though the heavy tarp of night was on my shoulders. I thought a moth that large must be a hallucination, a result of too much codeine, pot, and sake; however, I simultaneously thought it might be an old friend making the transmigration across the ocean of death, waiting for me to walk by in order to watch his impending rebirth. Two weeks previously he had died, and despite this it felt as though he was never here to begin at all. Still, in the midst of the labyrinthine streets

comprising the city, I knew he wasn't far away...
"Behind the door, that's where I'll be." Maybe I only
needed to nudge the door a little to see beyond my own
crazy doubts. I've often asked myself what do I prefer
more: night or day? When I try to weigh the virtues of
both I still find that I lean toward the night and the
shadows it brings, along with those unknown flavours
that skip over mind and tongue.

Night is when I see myself the most clearly, and if I'm
walking at night I always feel as though I can keep
moving forever in perpetual darkness and sweet silence.
There were days in the Western Quarter where I would
wander up and down the streets past the drunks and
junkies and feel completely free from the obligations of
existence. That kind of feeling does not come easily, nor
does it come often anymore.

Regardless, the night is always there for me when I need
it, pensively waiting for me to touch the hem of its silken
dress. So yes, the night is what I prefer.

*

Eastern Thought

After reading something like *The Tibetan Book of the
Dead*, or anything from Dōgen's *Shōbōgenzō*, the ideas

of Western religions fall by the wayside in comparison. Not so much because they are wiser or somehow better, but simply because they have a pureness and honesty that those Western beliefs lack. Now mind you I'm the first to admit, due in part to a basically Catholic upbringing, that so-called Christian ideals have had a profound influence on how I view humanity and the Universe. In saying that, I can point eastward and say the same thing about its influence and be completely honest by making such a statement.

Where did this begin exactly? I often point to my father's interest in the martial arts as that catalyst, for what I saw in the underlying philosophy of softness being greater than hardness appeared contrary to what I had come to believe by then, which prompted me to ask why that could be universally true. Eastern philosophy, in particular Taoism and Buddhism, often make reference to nature to show "what is" with its movements, transformations, and digressions with seemingly invisible effort, and how those smooth mechanics should be a reflection of our own actions and thoughts.

My interest in Taoism became even deeper when I encountered three books: *The Tao of Tai-Chi Chuan, Opening the Dragon Gate,* and *Chronicles of Tao.*

Within the pages of the book on Tai-chi I had a fine
introduction to the true idea of softness, as Tai-chi and
Qigong are considered soft-style martial arts that
demand a different kind of discipline that revolves
around stillness, ease of motion, and settling one's
consciousness. Easier said than done, but a path I've
dedicated myself to with an open heart. The rewards
every bit intangible as they are tangible, and I can say
honestly there are experiences in this realm of self-
cultivation that cannot be described, and should not be
described for that matter. Mystical insights— despite
Nietzsche's dismissal— have left their mark on my soul
and led me down a path of self-discovery...And is that
not the point, after all?

Opening the Dragon Gate amplified not only my need
for physical and mental cultivation, but also provided a
landscape for me to explore. If Christianity gave me a
basis in faith— another Nietzschean no-no, which to be
fair is correct in many ways from his perspective— the
Eastern teachings gave me a *tangible* system to work
with through the vessel of my body. The book itself is
the story of a young man who undertakes a sage's life
with three elderly Taoist adepts who utterly transform

him into the man he is today, over the course of twenty years of arduous esoteric practice.

And perhaps it is this idea of transformation that has transfixed me for so long that it has allowed me a certain kind of freedom and peace in a world swimming with sharks. Even the greatest books, however, like *Chronicles of Tao,* show us the struggle and disenchantment within the practice as well, with which I can clearly identify. The focus of that story, Saihung, looks at the world and longs for enlightenment yet realizes— at least from my vantage point as the reader— it cannot be forced, and our world is indeed cruel, giving him the will to move on and progress, because if we give in too much to our environment our hard work will be in vain.

This is the dilemma but also the challenge and maybe that is what Eastern thought has truly taught me: perseverance.

*

Hesse

1997 is the year I first heard the name Hermann Hesse and my journey to the East began in earnest. In the literary pantheon of my life, Hesse looms as one of the largest. Unlike Burroughs or Joyce, Hesse mesmerized me with content rather than style; with ideas rather than allegory. There must have been a huge rejection of Hesse in the late nineties as I found most of his books second hand, and it was with a copy of his masterwork *The Glass Bead Game* that I became more and more intrigued by what I personally saw as his turning away from Western values, or at least his character's struggle with Western values...something I struggle with myself.

Throughout his major works — *Demian, Siddhartha, Steppenwolf, Narcissus and Goldmund,* and *The Glass Bead Game—* we see the conflict of opposites played out in certain characters, or just an outright dissolving from reality, i.e. *Steppenwolf.* These were the remedy for my introspection when I first had the notion to write seriously, for they explored the conditions in how we must face ourselves and the society in which we live. I didn't care for the outside world then— at least the consumer, corporate monolith driven side— and I suppose I still don't, thanks in part to Hesse's work. His exploration of alternate faiths did nothing to hurt me either; as a matter of fact, it was refreshing to see a Westerner of his time and cultural background delving into Buddhism and mysticism. It's easy to see how the accessibility of his works came to such prominence here in North America thanks in part to people like Timothy Leary. Truly, in case no one believes it, literature can save a life...Literature, or just art in general can give a person validation when the world doesn't.

Perhaps that is the most amazing aspect of works passed down to us by the dead: the ability to have influence over so much for so long. For even if Hesse is forgotten (but I hope he will endure longer) centuries from now people may discover him as one might uncover hidden gems or gold. Now as I write in this frame of time, I can look back on those days where Hesse's words did more for me than a thousand prayers, and how words cast down over years, decades, or centuries beget words by another hand. As writers we probably don't think in these terms very often, for we're often consumed by our own need to survive.

Well Hesse, wherever you are, you helped me survive.

*

Drugs

Spring? Overcast for certain. The Irishman said to me with a smile and the skill of reverse psychology: *no pressure.* For close to an hour I thought about it— not with excitement or anxiety or even curiosity— but with the weight of a promise that I made to myself only a couple years before, which in light of my many experiences since then seem ridiculous: *I will never do drugs.*

But truth be told, I was at a low point in my life and I wanted— rather I *craved* a new experience. My home life seemed shattered due to my parents' separation and subsequent divorce, my marks in school were low, I was the target of assholes who thought they were cool, etc...So I said to myself *fuck it* and me and the Irishman walked in the cool air of spring and smoked some stellar hashish.

I came to really like hash. I liked the name even more when I began reading William Burroughs and he wrote about consuming copious amounts of majoun— a mixture of hashish and honey— during the time of the writing of *Naked Lunch* in Tangiers. The name too, I learned, was derived in part from the infamous *Hashishin* of the Middle East and their leader The Old Man of the Mountain, Hassan-i Sabbah, who famously said: *nothing is true, everything is permitted.* A signal of sorts for me to move into new territories of my mind. Of course, I didn't know that then, but the experience brought me closer to the world of writing, much in the same way it did for Burroughs who as a child imagined writers to be people that in his words: *"Smoked opium in Singapore, sniffed cocaine in Mayfair, and penetrated forbidden swamps with a faithful native boy."*

Well my situation didn't turn into a self-fulfilling prophecy like Burroughs, but the hazy, introspective buoyancy of the hash opened an inner doorway to the deeper self of dreams, imagination, and cold nightmares; not to mention a portal to unhinged laughter and bliss. Although within a couple years the Irishman disappeared from my life, the effects of his influence have been long lasting indeed.

Fast forward, circa 1999.... The appearance of the Ghost Hand.

The stupidity of youth walks hand in hand with the gravity of curiosity. Whereas hashish wasn't really about curiosity, the world of lower level narcotics did intrigue me, codeine specifically. But where to get this stuff? Anyone I did know in the so-called drug business was not interested in finding what I wanted. Now it's a different story since the advent of Oxycontin. But I digress.

What did occur could only be construed as either luck or divinely inspired. I err on the side of luck, seeing as though I don't really believe God wanted me doing narcotics in the first place. To make a long story short, I found a bottle of codeine pills in the rafters of a basement and then found the best time to do them in the comfort of my room during an overcast summer day, the pale glow of my desk lamp illuminating the keys on my electric typewriter. I sat on the edge of my bed with the bottle open, wondering how many I should take. Settling on four, I downed them and laid my head down on the bed. As my mind drifted, the body followed into numbness— a cool, comforting numbness that reminded me of ocean waves, white mist, and grey skies. At first I felt scared at the weight of my limbs and their hollow tingling until I realized it didn't matter: *my mind was liberated.* The stupor, however, was not the most interesting part...The resulting automatic writing of the ghost hand is what intrigued me most of all. My hand glided across the page, a consciousness of its own...I could merely observe as the words came in droves. Did those words survive? Yes, a few...most scattered to the wind or victims of the flame, but it was all worth it for a sentence of supposed substance.

Next came psilocybin. Friend? Not an enemy, but one might say an overactive acquaintance who became an ally. The kind of ally who shows you aspects of yourself that you were not aware of, and the kind of ally who takes you out of your comfort zone and into realms unknown, or at least to familiar places that become vaguely distorted. As cliché, and at the same time as sceptical as some might be toward the following statement, mushrooms opened my mind and altered my perspective forever. When I think back upon my experiences, few come back to me with the same clarity— strangely— like the ones I had with the magic fungi. Perhaps the greatest positive consequence was a renewal and even deeper interest in esoteric subjects. I woke the next day, even though I hadn't really slept at all, and gazed upon the rising sun with new eyes...All the chaos, flights of fancy, and hallucinations gave way to a grand clarity: I was renewed and changed for the better.

My appreciation of nature increased— looking at the night sky made me feel truly insignificant, and as I gazed at the flowers it seemed as though I was looking upon them for the first time. These intense experiences were repeated over the coming years, but with each subsequent experiment came more introspection leading me further down the spiral...

*

Agni & The Interzone

The fire burns out that way, crisp and clear. East, on the opposite side of Salamander Road, the graffitied walls, old tunnels, and the smell of hashish appear just as one may imagine they do in Tangiers. In the station: cold fluorescence and tall women waiting..."*loneliness is such a drag*" those eyes once said, in the same eerie way is how I remember it...The smoke and the heat amongst the slowly stirring light. I looked deeper as much as the light would allow, while the hands of evening covered a tepid wise man.

He said: *I'm looking for the crystalline clarity...I've been trying to as my cigarette drifts... You know where you are in the afternoon sun ... Where are you from?*
Me: *Here, just here.*

Quite suddenly and vividly, holding out his arms looking neither happy nor sorry, he pulled up his collar trying to hide from my eyes. The air was still crisp, the moon still bright...In the near darkness of the station, a forgotten corner, a woman...Her head, her palm, her shawl— beautiful winter over the distant whispers low and soft.

The Corridor is Daath: *the secret sphere of knowledge on the Cosmic Tree, the great Abyss.* That is the essence of Agni and the rest: uncertainty, unknown realms, a place of no returns...

*

Letter 3 (A long way from home)

The City in its ever-changing persona has taken on the dimensions of a labyrinth that grows infinitely more complex with the passing months. Do I even have a reasonable gauge of passing time since I was deemed *unstable* or *volatile* by some? Or does the possibility exist that I've achieved a grander sense of time and space? The days become colder; the sun icier and black; the trees sway naked on the narrow streets of the Eastern Quarter as I trample on the leaves. My work has only just begun in earnest. Some may call me crazy for trying to erect a temple out of stone, or rather out of my own mind, which in itself cannot be trampled over. Yet, as each piece is formed and laid down to grow, moving upward, my light knows no bounds. I was directed here by that same internal light, serving as a beacon to the world of my own dreams...a land of familiar ghosts.

*

Ramona A. Stone

Murder it would seem, at least in a literary context, has long been a central theme of literary art. A person needs only to turn to Dostoyevsky to see murder as something seductive and intriguing, not to mention beguiling and impenetrable to some degree. After 1864's existential *Notes from The Underground*, Dostoyevsky's major works focused on the many faces of murder, from political murder in *The Devils*, to parricide in *The*

Brothers Karamazov, not to mention his most famous novel *Crime and Punishment.* So, is it really a stretch of the imagination to think someone would try to elevate murder to the level of art in the real world? One such instance occurred in the late 90's— pre-millennium actually— when a private investigator was hired to look into the Art Ritual murder of Baby Grace Blue...

The private investigator, Nathan Adler, mysteriously disappeared sometime after 2001, which only served to thicken the broth. Strangely this story failed to make headline news, but if it were discussed today the world might not bat an eyelash. What makes this story so intriguing is the fact that the body was dismembered and carefully displayed with new additions, such as transistors, odd fluids, and other macabre inventions. The perpetrator took great care to place the internal organs around an art museum as well to further push the point.

Which brings us to the suspects: Ramona A. Stone and Leon Blank. Two lovers, two artists? Two outsiders? Adler never did manage to figure out if these two were behind the murder, but that hardly seems relevant as time goes on and Baby Grace becomes a distant memory.

History forgets the victims and always remembers the evil ones who do evil deeds.

Ramona apparently became an underground art dealer specializing in forgeries of every kind. Leon was shoved to the side at some point and ended up in a mental institution...or at least that's how the story goes...

The true order of the sequence: 5, 12, 17, 1, 2, 15, 16, 3, 8, 10, 6, 4, 14, 7, 11, 13, 9, 18, 19

*

Another kind of Fire, and the Movement of the Heavenly bodies

One only needs to draw the compass in order to know which way is the right path set out by the stars. Maybe that is what intuition is. She said to me— in the light of the moon during that early spring— *let your hand sketch your desires on my body, and let it move freely and naturally.* Far beyond any of my expectations I had of her or myself, we achieved something together despite the short time we spent in each other's company. Both of us were the pawns of fate, brought into a situation that pulled a shroud over us, only to produce a dolorous cascade of unimaginable feats in the end....

"*I am the whore and holy one. I am the mother and the daughter. The whore of a splendidly ingenious man. The holy one to a lifeless city; the mother of perfect deaths; the daughter of no one anymore.*" She said this as the candles burned low and then she seemed to vanish under the Lion and into the heat of summer.

No one is quite sure where he originated, but like many before him he was drawn not by stories or legends, but by a need to escape. Perhaps something inside him believed this walled city would suffice in bringing him peace. He carried the name of the Lion, and those who knew him best thought— perhaps strangely— that he had lived in Africa and spent many days and nights on the savannah. Though he never hunted game, he was known to hunt people. There are more than a handful of anecdotes that say he grew up in the famed Garden of Delights known only to the assassins who called it home for centuries. By way of the only means of transport— a train coming from the Outskirts through the only entrance and exit, the Marble Corridor— he arrived, a little weary and not entirely sure of his intentions. A world-weary face: blood-shot eyes, sun ravaged skin, tousled hair, along with a thick, slightly greying beard.

The locals— mostly booksellers and tea merchants— say he smoked heavily and had a very fierce intelligence. He became a pillar of mystery to the residents of the Dragon Court, and as the months slipped by in their presence, he became a fixture blending in seamlessly with his surroundings. Apparently one topic he repeatedly went back to when conversing with the many merchants was how the city transformed over time. One of these men cared to notate the following conversation in the attic above his store.

-No one from the outside, not even the Outskirts, can really know like a born and bred son or daughter. It's just impossible.

He pondered the comment for a moment and took a drag from his cigarette before responding.

-How do you mean? Philosophically? Physically?

-I would say both. Until you have seen what the city was built upon you would have little or no idea about what it is, let alone where it's *going.*

-So, I would assume you know the answer to the question then?

-Of course. But my knowledge came at a high price, just as anything worth knowing does...

*

Letter 4 (Butterflies)

To the Head of the Midtown Monarch Society...

Dear sir or madam, I'm writing to you with no clear intention as to my goal, but more than likely just to tell my story. Roughly two decades ago near Midtown's famous Observatory across the Velox, I saw peppered on one of the tall oaks a series of iridescent blue butterflies. What surprised me more than their appearance on that bright, cheerful day was their appearance in my dreams months later when the last leaves of summer had fallen...

Walking through a graveyard— which was unusual in itself— I saw off in the distance a crypt with a large bay window. Intrigued, I went inside and before me lay a closed coffin. One might think that fear gripped me at that point, but somehow I knew the coffin belonged to me. When I opened it, all that appeared was a fluttering blue butterfly.

Since then my life has changed in many ways, in much the same fashion a caterpillar changes when it emerges from the cocoon...

*

Door and Bridges (Again)

My progress through the myriad of rooms was really not progress at all. If I could describe the direct experience of walking through those neon blue halls (were they neon?), I could only compare it to traversing a foreign landscape, perhaps like journeying though the Atlas Mountains or skimming atolls on a raft and becoming lost. One of the rooms defied all the others in its geometry and content. A slab of marble, twelve sided, inscribed with Chinese characters...The floor a deep red, as though a series of blood sacrifices occurred just before I entered. Flocks of geese came to nest, appearing from out of nowhere then vanishing.

...Perhaps we shared the same inward gaze, and due to this fact it repelled us as much as it brought us together. I imagine that when the picture fades from view and all that is left is your own shadow, two options are available: give in to vice or walk with all your will into the maelstrom of chance.

*

Takashi Miike

Many people I know must think I'm fucked up. They won't say it to my face, mind you, but I'm quite certain this is what they must think. This stems from the kinds of books I read, the music I listen to, (which according to some is obscure and *nothing else interests me*), and the movies I watch. A lot can be learned about a person from the movies they find stimulating, in much the same way a great deal can be gleaned about a person by the kind of drugs they enjoy. In my case, the more I think about the kind of movies I enjoy, the less I know about myself, with one exception: Takashi Miike.

A quick note: This man speaks to the Opposite side of my spirit...that side associated with the Flesh, taste, smell, and elements of violence upon the Body. My introduction to his work, like many others was through *Ichi the Killer,* which one critic dared to call the *Citizen Kane* or *Casablanca* of splatter movies. The idea of opposites, so prevalent in Jung, Hegel, and Marx, seems to be a huge part of magick as well. The idea of equilibrium, or bringing into balance opposing forces is a necessity. That could prove to be an interesting theory.

Which brings me back to Miike. Perhaps my favorite Miike film is *Audition*, whose script was written by Ryū Murakami, who in some respects resembles Miike in his flair for the grotesque and unusual. The girl in the film— a seemingly innocent girl— named Asami, becomes the epitome of a kind of death wish in my mind: the leather smocked beauty who paralyses her victim like a black widow before inevitably killing them. These kinds of themes continually play out in Miike's films, and even though sometimes I should turn away, my head never moves...

*

The Vestal Virgins

The Virgins have been many throughout the years, and they have brought forth the Body. Not a *body*, but *the Body, the Equilibrium, the Opposite*. So, in a sense, yes, it's a physical presence that has manifested in my life. By name they are: The Girl of the Island, the Chessman, and the Conspirator. The Girl of the Island was a kind of elusive goal in those days when the nights seemed darker and the days seemed colder. Our afflictions were perhaps the same (existential sickness?) and we drifted about together until the ocean called her home again. A far cry from the ash grey walls of the hospital where I felt her cool lips on mine as spring began. And I recall years later crossing the barrier of water just to see her and leaving later that day and into the night feeling as though I would never see her again. All that mystery, all that perpetual possibility wrapped up neatly in my mind, and when I imagine her now, I know she is happy. That is the reward...

The Chessman is an enigma. A well dressed, intelligent enigma that buries himself in the world. Perhaps that is why I feel a great affection for him, but at the same time sense within him what I used to sense in greater amounts within myself: conflict. A brooding, coiled snake of frustration, anger, and a desire to reach out beyond the fringes. He is myself at the same age, only smarter and with a better sense of everything.

And as far as the Conspirator goes, he lingers in the back of my mind just like someone who would hide from the terrible world outside. His strength is his ability to absorb and listen to my words like no one else has, and vice versa. He is the man with the bag of dope, lost in the dream but ready with the rifle if needed. The hub of information and insight, laughter and seriousness, better days and smoke-filled nights.

They are the Body, the essence of a life I wish I led.

*

Letter 5 (The Mysterious Gate)

"There you will find the place I love the most in the world. The place I grew thin with dreaming."

Juan Rulfo

Midtown is a strange place isn't it? Since I was a boy, I often heard stories from various people that we are known for our disappearances. That walking the streets is a really an act of courage even for the common citizens who know the streets rather well. Oddly, no one ever asked the question why that is. Or has it been asked without me realizing it? Maybe that book needs to be written...maybe I saw its pages in a dream. Speaking of dreams, what do you see in the depths of sleep? Do you see the faces of unfamiliar people coming and going? Walls so high they seem to touch the very edge of space? I see all these things, over and over, as I walk these streets that never feel the same twice...Often I stop at the

Mysterious Gate near the Corridor and read the faded epitaph...

"*From the shore of life we depart and sail on the heaving waters of experience, arriving at the port of death and into our calm awakening.*"

*

Letter 6 (In the Annex)

There is an annex that connects the Old Library and the Hall of Records, linking two aspects of the past into a solid whole. I've often thought of civilizations passed where all the priceless notations became lost to time, people, or the elements and only the legends persist. This is what my intention is: *To create a legendary portrait of my former self as I disappear...*

(Lacuna)

Outside the annex. Third cigarette. Mind turning like spinning gears. Friction. The sky, once a deep blue, turns black...The sun a crimson dot...A flock of birds fly north then turn awkwardly east. I watch them until they vanish from view, then think that I too will soon vanish, only to be reborn again under more favourable circumstances by my own doing.

*

The Diary of Bastion Perrot, founder of Midtown

4 January 1810, Prague

Hanz and I gazed into the Vltava for a good portion of
the afternoon, our minds floating after three days in the
libraries, fingers caressing spines, making notes, and
wandering through the Jewish Quarter. The Great
Work avoids us and we've become tired. The New Year's
bells did nothing to renew us, but rather achieved the
opposite effect and dampened our spirits. Hanz readily
indulges in the local wares available to us, telling me: *It
feeds and hardens my resolve.* Though I can see in his
pale blue eyes— reddened by opium— that, he too, is
losing faith. The eternal sun gives me little strength even
as winter has done its best to kill me.

7 January 1810, Prague

I woke this morning to the sound of stifled cries and
moans from Hanz's room, where he spent the better part
of the evening with a prostitute he found near the tavern
we have been frequenting. Some habits take a lifetime to
break, and Hanz— despite his rare genius— indulges all
too often in the flesh. Myself, the hours were consumed
somewhat more delicately with the works of Basil

Valentine and that rogue physician Paracelsus, searching the pages for a guide to our goal— the Sphere, the Stone, the names are endless...

14 February 1810, Prague

Bitterly cold; bitter in temperament. Everything reeks of boredom despite being in such a beautiful city. Hanz has gotten wind of a small group of rogue chemists living on the coast of Portugal, who claim to have produced small amounts of gold. Perhaps we've been looking in the wrong places all this time when we should have heard the clarion call of the sea. In spite of our setbacks and wanton indulgences, I've come to realize that I'm missing something...something intrinsic and necessary that has evaded me since I left Germany two years ago. In my dreams I often see a shadow beckoning me...

18 February 1810

We left Prague two days ago by steam engine, the only passengers stuffed in a small compartment usually used for livestock, hoping to make our way west in a timely fashion, even though time is not really an issue. Hanz has begun having night sweats, terrible dreams, and sometimes violent shakes, leaving him with little energy to eat or converse. The only cure, he says, for what ails

him is the pale smoke from the opium pipe, which I told
him solemnly we had no more of and wouldn't for a long
while, prompting him to turn over in the near darkness.
As for myself, my energy is returning the further we go,
for the weather only improves. I read by a gap in two
slats of wood that let in a nice beam of light, often
softening my spirit, even though my thoughts rage with
an intensity so fierce I often lose sense of where those
ideas are leading. Night has come on fast, so I shall
conclude for now...

20 February 1810, the fringes of France
Arrived in the countryside of France late last night and
we decided to stay for a few days, trying to trace the path
of Flamel. The active pursuit of forbidden knowledge
has done much to unsettle me, for I feel doomed to
failure. Hanz, now slightly cured of his self-induced
delirium, has assured me our travels won't be in vain. In
fact, he revels in the thought that one day we will be
mentioned in the same breath as those we have studied.
Perhaps. He's becoming an egotistical braggart, who
despite this remains my closest, if not my only, friend.
He carries his confidence well, a little too well. Before
we began our journey out of Germany, he appeared more

enthused than myself at the prospect of uncovering the secrets written on the Emerald Tablet and the implications stemming from the possession of this knowledge. Now that zeal has captured me while releasing him...Though let it be said that he has done much to further our goals rather than hinder its progress. Maybe he does sense a breakthrough and has decided to let nature take its course. Time will answer everything.

22 February 1810, Night

Moving west again, only this time with some French cognac to keep us warm during the bone-chilling nights ahead of us. Hanz confessed to me this morning as we walked through the town square— tired and yawning due to lack of sleep— that he too has been haunted during the night by awful dreams. 'What do you see?' I asked. Putting on his bravest face he said: *"Large fires out of control in a place unfamiliar to me, in a country unfamiliar to me, with a thousand more people pleading me for help that I cannot give."* His face grew sombre. He set his eyes upon the ground and said nothing else. My deep intuition told me he was holding something back, but I dared not ask for fear of unleashing

something unpleasant within him. After a long silence
we both decided to give way to the weariness we were
both experiencing and hope our dreams would not betray
us again.

24 February 1810

We are supposedly in Spain according to the few signs I
see when we stop. Within a number of days we should
arrive on the coast. I've been reading Basil Valentine's
Twelve Keys this past week, trying to glean something
from its pages. One page in particular grabbed my
attention as Hanz and I shared a bottle of wine he
acquired from a young man during one of our rest stops.
It read as follows: *The two fold fiery male must be fed
with a snowy swan, and then they must mutually slay
each other and restore each other to life; and the air of
the imprisoned fiery male will occupy three of the four
quarters of the world, and make up three parts of the
imprisoned fiery male, that the death of the King will
be seized with a great love for the Queen, and will take
his fill of delight in embracing her. Until they both
vanish and coalesce into one body.* The appalling aspect
of the edition is there are no accompanying colour
illustrations,   leaving   me   with   a   rather   dismal

disposition despite my inebriation. Still, the vague notions of a tremulous growth comes from these readings of Valentine's. Hanz has not been reading much as of late but has given over much of his time to sleepy meditation, saying it brings forth wondrous bright light; a sort of antithesis to the nightmares which seem to be at an end.

28 February 1810, Lisbon

We arrived here in this splendid city only a day ago, and I'm already transfixed by its beauty. Our meeting with the chemist has been delayed as his mistress stated to us that he is "*deep in the midst of experimentation.*" The woman in question, Madelaine, seemed suspicious of me and Hanz even though she had knowledge of our arrival. She put us up in a spare room that overlooks the Tagus; the flowing water a soothing respite after the long journey out of the frigid winter of Prague. Our conversation with her continued long into the night, yet I could see that her generosity and easiness of speech covered a vibrant, untamed energy that flowed around her as though she could see into me without words. I felt unsettled. My growing drunkenness and the absence of our host only made me more anxious. Hanz, being the lustful rogue that he is, had his eye on Madelaine for a good portion of the evening, regaling her with stories of our time back in Germany and our many nights of debauchery around the town. She laughed at these stories, somewhat unsure of my participation in these activities. I assured her they were all true and Hanz was leaving out the most interesting details because we were in mixed company.

That made her laugh all the more. We asked when the chemist would be returning in order to greet us. Finishing her wine, she looked to the night sky and said it would be a couple of days before he would return, though she assured us he sent his warmest regards. Hanz did not seem at all fazed by the revelation, whereas I felt hesitant at the prospect of spending any more time in her presence despite her dark charm. We retired to our quarters where my companion quickly fell into a deep sleep. I spent a better part of the night staring into the Tagus, lost in thought, then reading by candlelight. Sometime near dawn is when I heard a knock at the door...

Diary Fragment

The Tagus glistens and I wonder if Hanz has slipped under the sheets with Madelaine after her visit to me earlier this morning. The house was almost irrepressibly silent, which tends to be quite unbearable for me in foreign cities...One does not know what spectres may lurk about in unfamiliar places. Perhaps I'm being slightly, what is the word? ... I cannot place it at this moment. One expects the master of the house to return today sometime in the early evening. I have no intention of returning until twilight. I bought a book to read, but my mind is not in the proper frame for contemplation. My only thoughts drift toward Madelaine. She is a very liberated woman; a little too liberated. Still, she has a charm that is strangely infectious. How her attitude will change once the master returns remains to be seen.

...Standing before the mirror she showed me the hand print Hanz had left on her neck, deeply set in her milk white flesh. She ran her fingers over the mark, feeling the residual warmth left by his palm. She tells me this as she removes the leather gloves and puts a blanket around her body, the opium still clinging to her aura...Her eyes hold a glassy sheen in the candlelight.

....

...The City has always had a reputation for violence and deviance— not to mention many strange and eerie disappearances— while in recent years the very fabric of extremity has been stretched beyond any recognizable bounds. Case in point: The Pavilion Arcade in the Dragon Court— so named due to the influx of Asian immigrants in the late 1800's— is today a web of intricate design carved from the finest steel. Metal lattices and archways weave through the air, pigeons coo and flap about, and the merchants within the Arcade deal only in herbal remedies and narcotics...A kind of dark Eden thrust between a Tigris and Euphrates of death that grew out of the arrival of Bastion Perrot...

"One who is afraid of fire will never command Salamanders"

Eliphas Levi

On the east side of Midtown, not far from the Dragon Court, is a cathedral that houses the remains of the city's founder, Bastion Perrot. This cathedral, long since abandoned and deemed a historical site by the local government, sits at the far end of what is known as

Salamander Road, where according to legend, Perrot walked through fire unscathed in what came to be called the *Ceremony of the White Salamander*, hence the name given to the stretch of asphalt that ends abruptly at that particular spot in the Eastern Quarter. Several historical sources— reputable, yet somewhat obscure— cite the ceremony as a test, not only of physical endurance of pain, but also spiritual essence and power. Perrot, a fervent explorer of the esoteric traditions, chose this cathedral— the first built in Midtown— as the location to push the limits of his newfound abilities* (*The Unknown Perrot*, Vol 1, Bergson. Midtown Press, 1900, pgs. 83-85). Another account says he performed this ritual naked as a sign of his 'birth' into a new realm of indestructibility, while respected Perrot academic Salizar notes he conducted this sacred rite with only one witness, who later propagated the story to the rest of his followers. The true identity of this person has not been ascertained.

One clue to the mystery of the *White Salamander* may lie in the hands of his closest acolyte and friend, Hanz Overbeck, who after Perrot's death quickly became not only the man to replace Perrot amongst his band of followers, but a key piece in the proliferation of his legend, albeit in the most subtle and secret ways* (*The Mystic Path and Midtown's Foundations*, Levitt. Golden Lion Publishers, 1926, chapters 1-5). Educated at Freiburg, Overbeck's interests were threefold: music, philosophy, and literature; however, it should be noted that he also had a penchant for wine and women, preferably together and in abundance. During one of his many orgies, it has been surmised through unknown means Overbeck came to be friends with Perrot, as only an *elite group* of members attending the university were allowed to participate. Perrot and Overbeck, both outstanding students and of suitable lineage, fit that criteria. One can only imagine what these two men talked about during those early years together in Germany, yet history tells us— even under the dim light of obscure sources— that a lifelong bond was cemented between them, and perhaps something far more undefinable as well...

As the years passed and their friendship blossomed, Perrot and Overbeck travelled Europe— some say into remote parts of Asia— accumulating a vast array of knowledge and experience that soon brought them to the attention of others who held similar worldviews; worldviews where the intellectual elite were destined to rule, perhaps in a similar vein as the philosopher kings of Plato's Republic. In many ways these two vagabonds were following in the well-defined footsteps of figures such as Da Vinci, Newton, and other polymaths. Giants whose ideas reshaped the heavens and earth. Though in the eyes of these two men— pursuers of the flesh as much as trekkers into forbidden knowledge— the need for control and power outweighed the mystical. For goodness, divine light, or anything remotely affirming did nothing to move them despite their Christian upbringings and rituals. This can be seen in their hidden handiwork that dances through the oldest parts of Midtown*. (*The Four Points and their Occult significance*, Cavellara, Dupont Editions, 1932, chapters 8-10)

The story as it goes surrounds the meeting somewhere near the borders of Portugal of Perrot and his future wife, Lilith— otherwise known as Madelaine de Garza— who played a pivotal role in grooming the man for initiation into mysticism. She was, as Salizar put it, "*an expert on the works of Giordano Bruno and Robert*

Fludd, famous alchemists and cosmologists of their day." A rumour also came to circulate that she was an adept in an obscure yogic school of sexual practices, something unheard of in her time. One can see that someone of Perrot's temperament— not to mention Overbeck's— would have an interest in this woman and the possibilities of a ménage-a-trois.

Perrot and Lilith were married in a Catholic ceremony near the coast of Portugal on the summer solstice of 1810. Salizar continues by saying that due to the duality of Perrot's nature, their marriage was undoubtedly consummated in a pagan fashion, possibly involving Overbeck. He concludes volume five with a lengthy discourse over the proposed significance of Perrot's cremation and the supposed scattering of his ashes in the four districts of Midtown. Surprisingly for an academic of his calibre, he gives no references or exegeses as to the validity of this event, and as such it has become an apocryphal tidbit.

Nothing turns out quite as we imagine. Either our ambitions are too grand, or we lack the necessary vision to see something through to the end. Such was the case with Perrot when he arrived in Midtown in the spring of 1812. Due to the vast wealth he inherited from his father, as well as his wife Lilith, whose family were French/Italian merchants of the de Medici bloodline, he was able to realize a deep-seated dream first imagined no doubt by the great Gothic structures and layouts of Europe's old cities. With the help of Overbeck, now highly versed in sacred geometry— evident in the public record where his letters are stored— various point of intersection came into existence in order to maximize what Perrot came to call the Great Sphere.

Perhaps it was no accident that years after Perrot's death students of occult science, here and abroad, found four of these points: The Old Library, the Observatory, the Pavilion Arcade, and the Marble Corridor were all on two key ley lines, indicating natural energy paths in the Earth. This discovery lead these same men and women to believe these markers play a role in what the locals call Midtown's "changing mask."

The story, one could say, is unfinished.

*

Letter 7

Hello Doctor...I've been making progress. One might even say I'm *cured,* if such a feat is possible. How is one cured from life without dying? During the past months I've continued to make changes in order to improve myself. You see, '*man is something to be overcome'* as Nietzsche pointed out, and I'm no exception. To bridge the gap between my current self and the next self is a huge feat— almost too huge— but *necessary* for people to understand my actions and, of course, my words in these matters. I have recently paid a former lover an informal visit that subsequently has forced me to write this letter to you, for nothing truly ends. All water flows toward the sea, which is consciousness itself.

*

Letter 8

...No doubt I find that in my moments of total clarity— in other words awakened to the world around me— I glimpse the edge of human consciousness where memory, desire, pleasure, pain, and everything in between solidify in a concrete whole, suddenly making daily life that much more exciting, but quite possibly darker. Have I ever fumbled in the dark? Awkwardly trying to find some important object only to trip and fall? Yes, I have. Though there are times when even the light fails us by showing us too much. Maybe what I'm saying is it's sometimes better to stumble and fall in the dark, for only then do we actually see.

*

The Trinacrium/Rainbird

Midtown/Murder: an argument for fringe art in the modern city, an excerpt.

"Throughout the millenniums, metals of all kinds— particularly silver, gold, and the like— were said to harbour a secret energy within them, allowing the adept passage through various psychological/ hallucinogenic states in various ritual settings."

Miss Black whispered to me, her silken hair damp from the rain: *"Wait for me there."*
Confused, I could only say: *"What?"* *"Where?"*
She said, whispering even lower this time: *"In the Pavilion Arcade."*

We were sitting in a lounge in the heart of the Trinacrium district, talking the usual talk of life, the

Universe, dead lovers, but this time she seemed distant, in a state of mental fog.

Again she whispered: "*I hate all this grit and grime— I want off this planet, like now.*" She downed half a beer in one swig and motioned for us to leave.

"*But we just got here. Don't you want to stay a little longer?*"

I could see by the look in her face that the rain of Midtown is where she wanted to be, with or without me. She walked out the door before I could protest at all...Finishing my own beer, I decided to follow her into the void of the Pavilion Arcade. She had a predictable pattern: a seat in front of an old piano tucked in the corner of the Leather Corset, a bar we often frequented together.

We had known each other a long time, and by ordinary standards we became inseparable for nearly two years, venturing into the night together, much like now, looking for some way to distract us from existence. A sort of metaphorical fever hit me when we first met, and the weather in my dreams became pallid— a total antithesis to the warmth and brightness I wanted. Really though, it was exactly what I craved: elusiveness, mystery, beauty all wrapped up in a neat little package of a person. The smell of damp flowers enveloped my nose as I reached the edge of the Trinacrium, where solemn groups of stoned teenagers stood outside dirty clubs to see unknown bands play loud and distorted. I could not see her, even though she didn't have a long head start. Off in the distance I saw someone whose features I could not make out, standing still amongst the growing shadows...Was it her? I can't tell you that, but as I slowly drifted forward I heard the street dogs awaken, their barks travelling up and down the streets and off the walls...

A singular scene flowed through my mind as the water pelted my skin...My face was young, nubile, almost virginal before I entered what they call the Marble Corridor...Out of the night, a large bird loomed, then the city seemed to wash away...

*

Scales

And so the Scales came into the picture to lie at either end of my reason, to balance my intellect and perhaps even my passions. Of course, the Universe was quick to keep that proverbial balance by placing one male and one female by my side. The Builder on one, the Secret Muse on the other. I met the Builder in the Old Library and conversation sprang from some unknown source, but in due time created a well we could drink from...

He: "What is your opinion on violence?"
Myself: I like violence, but in a rather comic book sense...an unreal way, really. I appreciate it in the same way I appreciate death, or something significant.
He: Hmmm, yes...a kind of video game fascination. In the land of the unreal anything can be loved.
However, one must tread lightly in the land of the unreal or you may never come back.

He was right. I never came back to reality (at least completely), and he never came back to the land of unreality. But he is always hovering there in the back of my mind, a perpetual possibility with the
Secret Muse. His words to me at the End of the Beginning of the End: *Remember Everything.* How could I forget? Those times with him and the Muse— her laugh, his laugh, her zest for everything, his intelligence for everything...

The Secret Muse: the cigarettes and short hair, the mischievous grin and great taste in music, the stories of LSD and the warmth and the hugs. I could carry one on each arm and they would balance me, as they should. Never too much, always enough, bringing out the best in me. I see now why we try to breathe life back into the past because of its familiarity to us, even though our picture of it fades as well.

Remember Everything, he said.
I keep trying, always and forever.

*

Nietzsche

When one finally decides to seriously start reading Nietzsche, they are truly stepping over a line. The line itself is the status quo, good taste, accepted views. To read Nietzsche is to step beyond these old concepts we have and hopefully beyond ourselves. He is a rarity amongst writers and thinkers I've encountered, if for no other reason he seems to bring everything to a halt. Reading Nietzsche is time standing still, the wind stopping, and feeling a glacial chill in your bones all at once. At the same time, the reader— if they are worth their weight— will feel okay to be human, if only for a brief moment.

What makes Nietzsche such a profound life experience, at least from my point of view, is the not the pronouncement of the death of God, or the Übermensch, but the fact that throughout his many books he brings forth the idea we can truly become more than we are as individuals and as a civilization. If nothing else, he *unsettles* our most deeply held opinions and makes us THINK. My uncle always seemed to be an admirer of his, though I'm not certain he ever read anything from his oeuvre. I can remember reading out loud Bertrand Russell's interpretation of Nietzsche from his *History of Western Philosophy* to my uncle during the summer of 1996, which turned out to be a crucial moment for me as I prepared to enter my final year of high school. From that subtle introduction I felt the power of that destroyer of worlds. I didn't actually start reading anything of his until my lunch breaks at a depressing job two years later, where the parables of Zarathustra gave me a new perspective on who I was as a human being. Nietzsche gave me *confidence* facing obstacles, pain, anguish, which around that time began finding its way into my life through insomnia, heartbreak, dysthymia, scattered thoughts, drugs, drink, and the night sky.

It would be too easy to find a quote relevant to this chapter, but I choose not to. I also choose to say nothing more of past struggles for the moment because they have passed. Only when those memories are digestible again can I turn toward the Void and accept my meal. For now, I thank Nietzsche as I would thank God, knowing the irony.

Amen.

*

The Flaneur

A lifetime of grey skies creates more mystery in Midtown than everywhere else, and a million sunny days had always been something absent from the horizon. A hideous autumn fell upon me, just like the ones I recalled from when I was young and roaming the empty streets, back-alleys, parkades, and those abandoned lots. When one is young a trip to the store at the end of the block is the whole Universe, and the lavender and cherry blossoms blooming are morning stars. I used to awake on Sunday mornings feeling an overwhelming sense of dread due to a heavy silence that made me think that the world had come to its end overnight. Slowly opening the curtain in my room, I glimpsed the thick fog covering Midtown. Only the tallest buildings stuck out of the top of its opaqueness, like black icebergs floating on a cloudy sea.

The nights wrap around me like a well-worn coat. My City moves without really moving. I've spent several nights walking past empty shop windows, drinking a little whiskey— an entirely innocent amount— and reading books under lamplight in the deserted, silent parks. Walking by the river I watch the slow-moving current, along with the occasional flick of a lighter or kiss on the High Gate Bridge. In *The Tibetan Book of the Dead,* when the symptoms of impending death are apparent, a white cloth is put over the face. The process takes nearly four days to extract the consciousness. The priest is left alone with the body and begins the chant, giving directions to the Western Paradise...

Why did I decide to come here? Too many long winters of heavy snow or weeks of torrential rain... floods...growing disease...influxes of burn victims from napalm...blackouts...every known calamity. I stand here on this balcony far removed from the balmy summer night blooming around me. Dozens of buildings dotting the landscape and they all resemble crematoria. Strangely these buildings are always near trains tracks, making my thoughts grow colder. Yes, the City resembles death, in much the same way the ocean reminds me of complete freedom and silence, or how the smell of ozone reminds me of being alive, so very alive. What will become of me?

*

Letter 9 (The 100th Window)

Have you ever looked through yourself? Through the layers, skin and all, to that place no one see but yourself? Many people— including you— have done your best to see that part of me in its entirety, yet I will go so far to say that *piece* can only be seen with the proper lens. Lately I've been devoting my time to widening the scope of that lens and directing it *back on myself* in order to see what is really in there. A better idea than sitting on an Italian leather couch watching a shrink scribble *observations* about what they think they see. This letter is kind of an informal goodbye; a farewell to all things systematic and neatly compartmentalized. I've departed from myself only to go find myself at my own leisure. Be well...

*

Alchemy

Nicholas Flamel. Paracelsus. Fulcanelli. These were the names that drew me inwards, closer to the truth. Closer to what I believed was the secret behind all knowledge. Since then, my world has not been the same, nor will it ever be. All roads lead back to Borges, and Paracelsus is no exception to that rule. I had heard the name before, but when a writer like Borges names a story *The Rose of Paracelsus*, I paid more attention. Mining the details of his life, one could see instantly he was an unconventional, mysterious man who perished under equally mysterious circumstances.

What made this story interesting— as well as a point of influence— is the fact he practised medicine and used plenty of occult science (alchemy) to influence his work. He famously said: "*Medicine rests upon four pillars: philosophy, astronomy, alchemy, and ethics.*" In short, he sought to integrate and solve, broadening the scope of his art while seeking to understand the fundamentals of nature through the Great Work of transmutation. His journey, his mystery, his view led me here to the contemplation of the Stone.

Enter Flamel, one of the most famous alchemists. Legend completely surrounds Flamel and his encounter with a mystical figure on the road to Santiago de Compostela. History says he achieved the twin pillars of alchemy: the creation of the Philosopher's Stone and the Elixir of Life; in other words, accomplishing the Great Work through both the wet and dry methods. What is most important here is not if these probably apocryphal tales contain any truth, but rather what they sparked within the minds of others and myself. The need for truth, the need for mystery and all its manifestations, and the need to seek leads us to the modern day.

Who was Fulcanelli? Ask the Brothers of Heliopolis...no one knows who they were either, but in Fulcanelli's second book *Dwellings of the Philosophers* was dedicated to them. The OSS, the WWII precursor to the CIA, searched for him because they too heard through the grapevine that a modern-day alchemist had seemingly achieved the same results as Flamel. Perhaps this all stems from a story where Fulcanelli's student

Eugène Canseliet used a projection powder to transmute 100 grams of silver into gold at the Sarcelles gas factory in France...Or that Fulcanelli came into contact with his student in the early fifties as a man of much younger appearance. To say the least, the story of this man who suddenly disappeared after digging into the very foundations of nature prompted me to learn more, absorb more, and create more. As the man himself stated when asked about the Stone: "*The vital thing is not the transmutation of metals, but of the experimenter himself.*"

*

The House, and the House on Ash Tree Lane

On Ash Tree Lane, there is a house whose inner dimensions are larger than the outside, as though the house was growing from within. I would have sooner lived in that house rather than the one I grew up in; no, that's not entirely true, but close. Memory dictates— as faulty as that mechanism is— that my time within those walls was often painted with darker shades. In one way it commanded a simple unpretentious beauty despite what occurred there behind the stucco, wood, and glass. My window faced west, and I often looked out upon the

midsummer horizon, or watched the rain fall in a
melody of crashes and applause. But mostly I looked out
the window late at night wondering when my dad would
be home, remembering all the times we drove through
the downtown streets late at night coming from my
uncle's optical company, eating cheap tacos and
doughnuts among the cab drivers, derelicts, and
strangers. In some ways our house was bigger on the
inside too, only when it came to the growth of absence,
fear, and anxiety that crawled under my skin and no
doubt my mother's as well.

That house stands as a bridge to a past I long for in a
sense, but at the same time would love to burn one day.
As the years go by, and the past becomes more obscured
by the movement of time and the details we impose upon
it, the pain fades too, by and by. Yet it was a strange
pain: a pain that makes you despair but also hopeful. A
pain that you want to erase forever, but carry with you
in the palm of your hand like an umbrella.

The sound of low weeping...curses...smashed dishes...the
smell of vomit and loud records, television
blaring...aroma of fear, the shattering of glass...the
flipping of cards in a state of perpetual solitaire... locks

being turned in the wee hours...mysteries...charcoal burning under the tapping of raindrops... dog and cat asleep together as friends...no heat...empty rooms, awake for days listening to the movements of mice...walking on eggshells...reflections in the mirror...phone call in the night...taste of raspberries...sand in my shoes...

Days seemed shorter, the sky grew more ominous, and eventually Son and Mother left. With keen eyes and fearless intuition one may come to understand a profound event in his/her life, and with that new understanding finally hold onto something which was once hard to grasp... I went another way (I think): read more, listen, watch, walk away...

*

Films

Cinema mostly passes me by now; in a haze of images and terrible soundtracks the world of film becomes more distant. This is not something one person wants to hear or accept: he may be listening. Despite this fact, my thoughts wander over celluloid more than they should, and I begin to wonder how a core group of filmmakers have tapped into my subconscious so thoroughly. Not that it matters, does it dear reader? Art is a lie, right?

Akira. I mention this film first because each time I've watched it the pit it creates in my stomach and the hole it burns in my mind gets larger. The core 'message' is undecided, but the theme of unusual transformation, the essence of death, and eternal life are subverted into a steely coolness, sticking to the grey matter. Despite its weirdness, violence, and epic grandeur, a sense of hope comes over me by the end, rescuing me from my thoughts that surely have entered a hellish place. Regardless, it has a place dear to my heart, even if to think of it is to confront subjects best left for the dead.

Apocalypse Now. There is a shortage of cheery flicks in my collection, and this one is no exception. This is a film that *changed* me, as I'm certain it changed many others. It fundamentally altered the way I look at human nature, war, hypocrisy, and quite possibly life itself. Even to view it purely from an aesthetic point of view is to see near perfection: superb acting, amazing cinematography, incredible sound design...But in essence my favourite parts are Captain Willard's one-sided conversations with Colonel Kurtz, where we the viewers finally get to see 'the heart of darkness'. Art doesn't always need to be profound to change us, it only needs to be there for us at the right time. Though in this case, being profound in every way can only enhance the ideas it wrestles with from beginning to end.

The Films of Cronenberg and Kubrick. A gap in memory dictates my initial encounters with these two filmmakers are forgotten, though truth be told, the images— but more importantly the *emotions*— are what push me back to their films. Great filmmaking, like great literature, always bring you back because that sense of unresolved conflict or underlying tensions/ mysteries are almost perpetual in nature, ever expanding and changing our opinions of what we have viewed. Kubrick's *A Clockwork Orange* and *Eyes Wide Shut* still create an inner dialogue when I watch them, just as *Dead Ringers, Videodrome,* or *A History of Violence* by Cronenberg do the same. Despite my dislike of repetition in most cases, Cronenberg has done the most with repetitive themes— sex, violence, the body— that they create sublime variations demonstrating the true universality of these themes. Both are geniuses at this, despite what my detractor might say.

David Lynch. To categorize David Lynch is a near impossibility, simply because his art defies the usual parameters of filmmaking. On the surface, one sees familiar motifs from classic film, but beneath this— dare I say, artifice— lies the true story. But what is the true story? Like Kafka— who I was pleased to learn was an early influence on Lynch— his narratives create a strange horizon that point toward something I'm sure only he can truly understand. Of course, any new vistas that the viewer is challenged by are the product of truly great artists. If I *had* to pick just one Lynch film it might be *Lost Highway*, but *Blue Velvet* or *Mulholland Drive* stand on equal footing. I'm never bored by him. Even Michael Haneke. I could go on about filmmakers, but who would listen? However, in closing I will say that the films of Michael Haneke are brilliant meditations. Find out why and get back to me. The words I could choose to describe him would do no justice. He is someone to experience, not to talk about, just like the others already mentioned.

*

The Nexus

"Synchronicity is an ever present reality for those who have eyes to see." Carl Jung

...1997. This is perhaps where the thread began, leading me into the labyrinth that I have yet to emerge from in one piece. To be honest, a part of me never wants to find my way out...

The name Carl Jung came up during a philosophy class I was taking in high school, which incidentally was being taught by my English teacher, Mrs. Richardson— a dedicated Jungian and lover of the works of Hermann Hesse, who in his formative years became familiar with the Swiss doctor. The name stuck, and my excursions to the library became more frequent.

Fast track, circa 2007

The air became thick, hard to breathe. Mind racing, only this time it felt like it did a handful of years before, yet this time it was different— deeper, stranger, scarier. No, this was not the same anxiety I had experienced before in waves...This was the wave itself, the very eye of the storm...a phenomenon I've come to call the Nexus. I had stepped into an extraordinary realm, but a realm I barely understood.

Even now, I feel as though I know nothing about its true reason for manifesting itself at that point in time. Here is what transpired: basically, I thought I was on the verge of going insane, due to the number of synchronicities appearing in my life on a daily basis. Not one or two, but sometimes half a dozen a day, conveying and creating a theme in my life that resembled an intricate web of connections still multiplying today, though now it's numbers rather than events, people, or places becoming the dominant piece of the puzzle.

How did this begin? Too much weed and mushrooms? Classic over-thinking? Reading, writing, deeply dreaming too much? What? In a small way, I see it as a combination of all those things...How else does one *explain* foreseeing outcomes in films before you watch them, or having your friends look at you strangely when synchronicities start happening to them when only you're around. So yes, inevitably a sense of dread and the idea I was going insane weighed on me...did anyone notice? Did I ever mention it? Maybe. But even in the midst of such an experience it's hard to be objective. The twisting and odd connections between people and events appeared to be larger than life, as though a small fissure in time and space opened, allowing me to see the great expanse it was hiding. For the first time since I was a boy, wondering about the mechanisms of existence, did I actually realize I might not be insane after all.

*

Letter 10 (Shadows)

One should play among beautiful people, or at the very least look inside them with an honesty that one looks at oneself with in order to see what is truly there. I direct this toward you again my dear. Who else but you would listen even though a voice inside your head tells you not to? Did you ever look past the surface of my actions to *see* how I truly felt about our time together? Silly question. All you will recall is how I managed to strip the layers off you without much effort and without stripping off mine. Still, the nearer I get to my final departure— away from Midtown, not life— a certain truth has begun to overcome me like a person who was departing from life, knowing this is an opportunity to open up and reveal. Did I ever mention the shape and dimension of your shadow when I saw your naked flesh under dim light? And what do I mean by shadow exactly? Do I mean the velvety blackness on the wall as you reveal yourself inch by inch? In some way, yes, but something more beyond the tangibility of your flesh and the pleasure I received from it on so many occasions. That 'something' I speak of used to come to life on your face as you smoked a post-coital cigarette— a kind of deep anger or frustration. The kind of expression that made me want to see into you more in a way than sex can, even at the best of times. Maybe you saw something similar in me, and rightly so...something unsettling, perhaps even *unholy*.

Take care. Mantra....

*

Vayu and the Istanbul

The Vayu. The Scorpion. We knew each other for a long time— a very long time, as a matter of fact. On those tired midsummer afternoons we would walk the streets of the Vayu/Istanbul district, usually looking for a bookstore that we could loiter in and find some relief from the stifling Midtown heat. The Scorpion, sweat pouring off his brow, asked me in an almost hushed tone why this area was called the Istanbul...I said I believed one of the founders was inspired by the architecture of Istanbul and tried to clone it, but in a more Western fashion. His name was Overbeck. Looking casually around he said, in an even more subdued tone: *"But nothing around here looks even vaguely Turkish. Doesn't that seem strange to you?"* It certainly was true: nothing physical seemed to bare the mark of the Hippodrome, the Grand Bazaar, or even any reference to districts, the Bosphorus, or people associated with that Celestial city that connects two continents.

Perhaps, I said meekly, he associated Istanbul with wind. This part of town (The Vayu) has a strong association to air, the breath, moveable energy. The Scorpion turned to me, the glaze of intense heat reflecting off his face, nodded in agreement but added: *"Of course, one can't ever be sure of what influences an artist, that is far too personal and obscure. We can only guess, no matter what they may say about where their influences come from. To me my friend there are only two things that truly matter: Sex and Death, beginning and end."*

Orhan Pamuk, writer and native of Istanbul his whole life says: *"Sometimes one's city can look like an alien space. Streets that seem like home will suddenly change colour."* This has always been the case with Midtown, forever appearing one way then changing masks. Then I ask myself what can I be sure of in this moment?

*

Eroticism

The role of the voyeur is the reflection that I see in the mirror; or to put it another way: the voyeur is the *other half* being chased by the one *looking* in the mirror, thus creating perpetual cat and mouse game where one is always studying the other. Windows, doors, locks— behind all of them lies the ideal image of sweat, skin, silk and all that is sensual. Hermann Nitsch, black tape, the blowing of curtains on a warm evening in spring, those too, fit in the same category. Pin and needles, restraint, the gloved hand reaching for the face, smiles in the semi-darkness, or the cryptic blueness of approaching winter. The thought or presence of a knife or sword, dagger, razor twisting around in the palm or scratched across the skin...

...I turn my face away from the glass and light a Javanese cigar, trying to dream of her as the smoke circles my head. Maybe that's why I came here, even though I knew she was right about the pain. A dull sensation sitting behind my heart...The city begets symbols that prove we'll never escape what inevitably comes for us all. I begin with death and try to remain humble.

Curvature of the breast...exotic flowers and butterflies...wax masks and pretty tattoos...behind lace and stockings, never revealing the dimensions of the hidden city. Yes, black lingerie: a reminder of a thousand other snapshots from models and pin-ups, saints and whores, finding their way through ought tunnels and materializing in the mind's eye...

We're all under the impression that what is familiar will always be in the same place— yet one comes to understand very quickly that everything is moving and those tried and true visions or spaces of comfort move and disappear too...Including her.

*

Alcohol

Praise the juniper berry. Praise hops and barley. Praise all the malt, all the sour mash, those fermented grapes, and the sugar cane. Heap praise on it all, for it makes us happy before it makes us sad. Or as Jack Kerouac said once: *"Never get drunk outside your own house."* I think that was actually one of his rules of writing, and perhaps, his most poignant point. I would like to say years of inebriation has brought me some splendid insights into human nature, but on the whole it has really been a low point. Sure, sure, friends will paint a different story about all the fun times had at pubs and around the campfire, which are all true, but I can't forget at least four occasions where it made me feel lower than an ant at the bottom of a canyon. That is a terrible feeling— a feeling of abandonment, loneliness, and hopelessness as the night or the overcast sky tosses its massive weight on your mind when your mind is already heavily weighted...The Universe seems empty, or rather: *you feel empty.*

Despite this, I continued to drink until the world shrank away. Now, let's not be hasty and assume that I was or am an alcoholic. Quite the contrary, actually;

however, truth be told I liked to binge. Didn't this come across? Ah yes, too busy talking about the evils of drinking and the pain it caused. Still, there are nights as I'm lost in thought looking out the window or reading like an uncommon person and the deep desire to down a bottle of Bombay gin creeps into the blood. When my body begins listening, the Shadow rises to meet those thoughts and begins that usual dialogue I've come to recognize over the years as a war for my soul. Perhaps this sounds a tad melodramatic, but yes, I'm at constant war with myself over a great many things, so fucking get used to it, all right?

Who wins in the end? Usually my better reason does...As a friend keeps reminding me, half-jokingly and half seriously, "*You have a family.*" Yes, yes I do have a family and if I didn't for the sake of argument, I'd be sure to let the beast out of the cage for a while. But the fact is I *do* have a family and I love them. Say cheers anyway and put my attention back where it belongs: on the book sitting quietly on my lap.

*

Archers

...The Archer fires an arrow across the city. He pulls up in his dark silver car and tells me to get in with a smile. We exchange greetings and pleasantries and he clumsily lights a cigarette. Off we go.

"*Where to?*" he asks.

"*Wherever,*" I say.

The night is young, we are young— the roads are glittering with the paths of fading neon and the air is fresh and alive. Somehow we always end up in a place where light is virtually non-existent and I feel as though the external world is no longer there to berate us. Haze of smoke, weird thoughts, laughter, maybe even a little despair thrown in for good measure, beating out a rhythm and cascading into nothingness...

He asks me slowly after his fourth beer: "*We should smoke a bowl, right?*"

Yes, always yes to this question— one, two, maybe three bowls. Stoned for Eternity, passenger in the silver shuttle screaming across time and space, never to return. Then there were those long walks... hillside drunkenness, stargazing, stupidly ranting and raving as though the whole galaxy could hear us...only echo. We fiercely attacked whatever we could. Pissing on the faces of politicians then tossing their cardboard visages to the wind, laughing in unison as we stuck it to *'The Man'*, elated by our minor disobedient natures then passing out shortly thereafter, perhaps dreaming of darker times when the Devil meets you in those spectral cities of your mind.

Times of blackness— too much beer and blunts, pills— numb, listless, listening to God knows what while sitting on old chairs, barely able to speak. Those are the best times that hover just close enough to touch, never escaping our reach amongst a thousand others.

And yes, there is a second shooter on the grassy knoll of my Path, the Strange Saviour. The man who appeared in my kitchen one day and never left. Who ate meals with me, who shared a beer or two with me when the light of summer seemed fresher, the air lighter, and my hopes seemed less dim. The man who would never say no, but expected nothing in return other than a little respect. The man that would rant and rave, carrying on into the wee hours hunched over a field of battle, shaking the dice in his hands...But he would also let me rant and rave and carry on, challenging me, teaching me the ins and outs of world history, recent history, serious history as though it pained him to do so...

Laughter, always laughter, despite it all. Talk of falling stars on the Nile only seen by Egyptian eyes, the towering monoliths of *2001*, sounds of Floyd and Zep on the stereo, and a trail of smoke from a thin joint. That is what is fond and memorable. No lack of love from someone who wasn't flesh and blood...Now bruised and virtually silent, immovable, in the tiny room with curtains made of bedsheets, eyes closed and laughter subdued.

I don't want that to be my final memory.

*

Albums of Fury

A thousand lights in a darkened room, ANS, The Remote Viewer, Time Machines, Black Antlers, Music to Play in the Dark Vol 1. The price of existence is eternal warfare. Coil: To me these six records destroyed the boundary between music and artistic intent and combined the two together in such a way that it still astounds me now. In other words, making one's actions in life synonymous with the art and making something new and exciting— or in this case, dark but oddly life affirming. The depths of these albums are not for the faint of heart, but only for those willing to step outside themselves and document their thoughts and actions after listening. Danger. Beware.

Tim Hecker. *Radio Amor.* But really anything from his catalogue.

Music in some ways has had a more profound effect on my writing than books have— especially music of the electronic variety. Brian Eno, who in my humble, very biased opinion, is the supreme genius of mind-altering sound, creating such a wide spectrum for others to delve into that the results have been staggering. Tim Hecker, whose sonic tapestries are draped in static, molds a world similar to Eno's in terms of mental stimulation and emotional depth, though in such a way it defies description. A good friend introduced me to Hecker through the record *Harmony in Ultraviolet,* but it was the tracks *The Shipyards of La Ceiba* and *The Song of the Highwire Shrimper* that whetted my sound palette off of *Radio Amor.* Around the time of those first listens— along with an increasing tendency toward absorbing experimental music— I began to finally

believe I could create music myself. It was, and
continues to be a wondrous feeling.

Talk Talk. *Spirit of Eden/Laughing Stock*. One word:
beautiful. Thank You N. For this. Perfect timing,
perfect bliss. Nothing more can be said...

Oren Ambarchi. All records. If there is an undisputed
king of experimental minimalism in modern music, it's
Oren Ambarchi. *Suspension* gave me a concept of pure
tone and musical abstraction, but more than anything
else it gave me an opening: a tiny tear in space in which
to evoke the cherubim of imagination and unusual
forms of thought. Music must not only entertain—
despite the fact that many believe that is its only
function— but it must also give way to something bigger
and more important as well, whether it be emotional,
psychological, or even physical. Ambarchi's records
work on at least one of these levels to such a high degree
that I know only of one equivalent, but I'm not going to
say who. Just listen.

Stereolab. *Cobra and Phases Group Play Voltage in the
Milky Night*. Stereolab is the perfect example of what
pop music could be if it actually cared to have depth. The
Beatles— dare I say the boy band of their day— as time

progressed managed to transform their sound without disregarding the pop sensibility they had created. Listening to *Cobra* I'm convinced they spend a huge amount of time honing a sound that is catchy, yet at the same time musically and artistically relevant. This can probably be said of all their albums, though songs like *The Free Design* continue to stimulate me just that little bit more than the rest. Too bad we may never hear more from them in the future.

Mono. *Under the Pipal Tree*/Boris *at Last-Feedbacker*. Just like Talk Talk I'm not going to say anything more than is needed: spectacular, dizzying, dark, expansive in ways I didn't think possible. Here in the West we need to pay closer attention to places like Japan and the diamonds they keep mining. As a culture I know of no one richer and stranger...maybe the French.

In conclusion: Black Moth Super Rainbow. I imagine this is the kind of music I'd be creating if I grew up in a forest and did a lot more psychedelics while listening to *Tangerine Dream* while covering myself in mayonnaise. Brilliant...

*

Yukio Mishima

"How dearly indeed I loved my pit, my dusky room, the area of my desk with its piles of books. How I enjoyed introspection, shrouded myself in cogitation with what rapture did I listen for the rustling of frail insects in the thickets of my nerves."

The first book of Yukio Mishima's I read was *The Temple of the Golden Pavilion*, which I found to be very interesting, but not as interesting as I found the man, who lived out a personal philosophy to the end, the very End. Not that I believed his novels to be mediocre. What they symbolized to me were successive steps toward annihilation while at the same time demonstrating a perverse view of what is beautiful. For those that don't know the Mishima story, he committed ritual suicide (seppuku) after a failed coup d'état of sorts shortly after completing his masterpiece *The Sea of Fertility*. Those four books encapsulate the essence of his personal philosophy in a literary medium, but it was the higher ideals of action that he is ultimately remembered for decades later.

Besides the *Sea of Fertility*, two of his non-fiction works had the biggest impact on me: *Sun and Steel* and *Yukio*

Mishima on the Hagakure. The quote at the beginning of this section is from the former book, where Mishima at mid-life was creating his *crisis* that proved to be his greatest moment. The book in my opinion is a renunciation of literature in favour of the tangibility of the flesh through his obsession with body building, kendo, and homoerotic death— the idea of leaving a beautiful corpse in a wake of blood and torn skin became the antidote for a life fraught with the unfulfilling nature of literature despite the life he breathed into it with brilliant insight.

When I finished *Sun and Steel* all those years ago, the possibility of leaving behind literature seemed ridiculous, almost unthinkable. Words sustained me like nothing else, they are the portals that lead everywhere, but as I've come to realize over the years, they also obscure our view of the personal horizons on which our fate lies. Roberto Bolaño— another author who faced the void, albeit with a more humorous twist— hoped that literature was not a way of delaying things, but I'm almost afraid to think it may be true. Literature keeps us pleasantly distracted even as we inch closer to the end. Perhaps Mishima realized this at the perfect time and created with the sword, not the pen, the perfect end. I, too, hope to find my perfect end...

*

Mitsuko, the Baphomet

...I stand before the mirror (slightly cracked in one corner and still gleaming with condensation), naked as the day I was born, unaware of how much of *me* is actually *him*. Where does he end and I begin, and vice versa? I can almost hear the confusion (insofar as confusion can be heard across invisible channels) and I sensed his presence in the girl he first kissed, or in a moment of soft radiance, maybe even in those grey dreams of quiet city blocks. A brightness follows him and he doesn't even know it yet...A brightness that is twofold: one being his potential, and two, me his anima.

The sky is opaque and all that is left here are remnants of a cocoon: a few books, scribbled notes, dried bits of cheese. Walking back into the bathroom, I run the water until it's warm and splash some on my face...My hair is getting long...my eyes are puffy and red...

....

I wait by the stairs hoping she will show, absently watching people on Salamander Road. My skin itches as she comes into view...Her hair perfectly straight and tidy and a nicely patterned dress adhering to her hourglass figure. One faces the landscape in front of them in much the same way one faces themselves at a crucial moment: should I move forward? If the scenery is beautiful one does not hesitate; facing ugliness is another matter entirely.

I've often dreamt of the Apocalypse, and one has to wonder if the future is really projected through our subconscious. The ability to *see,* as Castaneda put it, can leave a person lonely and frustrated in a world so consumed by illusion. When I was young, I twice saw the apparitions of the dead... What will become of me? I crave the silence of the abandoned city...As she gets closer I recall the words of Nevin Batista... "*What is in a glance? What composes such a simple intriguing gesture that leaves people feeling so ambiguous?*"

*

Cuisine

Life seems totally not worth it without great food, am I right? Some may disagree, but whatever... *you know* I speak the truth. Nothing will ever be a bigger addiction in my life than food. Bigger than alcohol, drugs, sex, books, music, etc. And not just because it sustains a person, but when I think *deeply* about food and its origins, it seems like an amazing story in and of itself. From the beginning when fire was a new concept and not just a novel idea, the world of cuisine was born and the magic began...I mean, one can only imagine what it was like to eat the first piece of cooked meat over an open flame, and then eventually season it and make it taste even better. Like anything, I'm sure this was a lot of trial and error, but it's amazing to think it was a conscious act, setting in motion something unbelievable.

Smell is the sense most closely tied to memory and of course it's easy to see food being a great part of memory. Aromas rising from kitchens, whether it be my mother's, my Babcia's, or even one of my aunts, gives way to items such as chicken cacciatore, homemade perogies, or strawberry and rhubarb pies. It's memories such as these that are always tinged with happiness; memories that waft and hang in the air, so real and tangible you feel as though they can be touched...And, if you imagine them hard enough, the taste is still on your tongue. Of course, eating is synonymous with dining out, and many of those memorable culinary experiences begin and end there.

Take for instance the Old Diner in the Western Quarter, where I would eat monstrous hamburgers coupled with waffle cut fries seasoned with a special spice that still eludes me as to what it was exactly, while listening to the jukebox as the sun danced over Salamander Road. And how could I forget all those tired afternoons in the arcades eating pizza subs slathered with too much sauce, drinking Tahiti Treat, and putting me on a huge sugar high. As I gained momentum as a teenager, motivated by my stomach and exploring the streets of the Dragon Court, other Shangri-La's appeared before my eyes: the billiard hall, now dead and gone, that served the best Wor Won Ton soup I've eaten with its generous slabs of barbequed pork and a dozen wontons in a salty broth. To me that was heaven on Earth, and perhaps it still is even though the area has morphed into a horrible rendition of itself.

Before the monuments to capitalism arose around Midtown there were places like Galaxy Donut, with its strong coffee and epic éclairs I gorged myself on. Éclairs I haven't tasted in decades, for the same reason wontons no longer dance in my mouth: progress. I've taken into consideration why I rarely walk at night anymore and I've come to the conclusion that there are no new smells to entice me. No that is a *lie*, maybe the worst lie. I say to myself: *Don't conceive of a future where you are hungry.* Sadly, I do conceive of such a future in my weaker moments, and if I pause to reflect on all those untold millions who have nothing to eat at all, I've already lost my appetite...

Letter 11

This is a sort of farewell as much as it is a letter letting you know I'm doing well where I am now, far from the crowds and mysteries of Midtown. My room is sparse, almost spartan in a way, but I find it next to impossible to completely rid myself of books, music, and the occasional prostitute. Suffice to say that I'm comfortable and planning my next move despite my quotidian routine at the moment. What is my next move you ask? I'm not entirely sure of my motives at this point, and

besides an overwhelming *philosophical* motive that
continues to grow in a bizarre way each and every day
between hours of extreme despair and creative highs.
I've once again found my calling, which can only
continue to find its way to actuality within the flesh of
humans. Does this make any sense to you? My artistic
vision, as one might call it, is quickly becoming a twofold endeavour...In one respect with the pen, and the
other with the sword...

*

5 Conspiracies of Interest

1: John Titor, time traveller, predictions of civil war and
economic collapse and the inevitable remaking of
mankind in a new image. Seems outlandish, right? No
one travels through time to see our future... a grim
spectacle is what the answer seems to be. Besides, I know
who John Titor is.... You only need to watch *Stein's Gate*
to know the answer. True or false? Most likely false, but
who's to say?

2: The Philadelphia Experiment. Leave it to the powers
that be to take the ideas and technology of a genius like
Tesla and use it for nefarious— I'm guessing here—

means to bend time and space. Some sort of relation to the previous entry perhaps? True or false? True. It seems to be the idea of reckless, power hungry rulers to grab all the knowledge for themselves, leaving the majority in darkness.

3: The Moon Landing. The Other Sphere has always been a mystery— a heavenly body that enchants us as much as the Sun. The anomalies and history throughout the ages seem to point toward a deep fascination. Why wouldn't we want to go there and claim it as our own? True or false? True, but I'm going to have to side with Jay Weidner on this one: we went there but not when we say we did, nor was our mission what it supposed to be. NASA has a checkered past too profound to think otherwise.

4: The Bilderberg Group. A secret yearly meeting of some of the richest, most powerful, and influential people in the world gather to *speak freely* about *what needs to be done*. Media blackouts, very heavy security, no records of conversations or discussions, all behind closed doors. True or false? I heavily lean toward true, if for no other reason it's so shrouded in secrecy and by the powerful people who attend. What better way to enslave humanity further by meeting away from the common folk. Rule by secrecy and shadow.

5: 9/11. I'll never forget what I was doing that day or who told me the news, but more importantly I'll remember the haunting images, the people jumping to their deaths, clouds of ash, and the sense of impending doom that gripped me. True or false? With all the overwhelming testimonies, countless experts bringing forth data, the wealth of inconsistencies, and the subsequent events that sprang from it, I have no doubt that this conspiracy is true, to the detriment of everyone.

*

Auster

Anyone who reads with any kind of zeal inevitably comes across books that change their life, or at the very least change their perspective on life. In the case of Paul Auster, he manages to do three things: change my life, change my perspective, and at the worst of the three, change my opinion of him (however brief)...

He is deceptively simple in his approach, but his works are embedded with a constant unknowable factor, which may often leave the reader scratching their heads. I always feel as though I'm being deceived somehow when I read his books, or some calamity of fate awaits me at the next turn of the page. This isn't a menacing feeling, but a feeling precipitated by chance; a sense of the world churning out endless mazes and coincidences that have you questioning the characters and their place in the whole scheme, and as a reader, your place as well.

In the *New York Trilogy* there is a line from *City of Glass* that resonates with me: "*New York was an inexhaustible space, a labyrinth of endless steps...It always left him feeling lost. Lost, not only in the city, but within himself as well.*" When I finally made it to New York in 2002, I understood what he meant by the inexhaustible breadth of the city, but I never felt lost. I felt almost at home on the streets that lead everywhere and nowhere at the same time. Though I haven't travelled widely, the only place I feel lost is my own city; I feel lost in myself, too. Out of all his books, that one taught me the most about my own identity and how we are tied to the places we love the most, even if they are not metropolises like the Big Apple. The familiarity of our surroundings turns us inward. Even at his weakest moments, i.e. *Timbuktu, The Book of Illusions, Travels in the Scriptorium* he still gets me to finish his books. He also has the somewhat dubious honour of being the only writer I'll always go back too even if he disappoints me. In some ways he is like a literary father, but that is another story altogether.

*

Poets

...We no longer have the fever that was fanned by the vortex flames and the new silence. This is the evening of the explorers, taking you into the dark...Everyone yelling 'fashion forward', watching a communion of hope, bodies restored, rain and spirit, owning their ignorance.

End of an age, but let there be decency for the lightning and stranger that will surely burn you. Little fanfare for the art slaves over a panorama of grace— a burden of ashes are really a burden of stars— dazzling and falsified...

They know our faith, deceiving the beasts. Unmasked, drunken. Vigils, violence, science and pattern writing letters stating their courage, their knowledge, lifetimes wading through puddles created by heavy rain sent by

God's serenity. Deported, dispossessed between imaginary borders, earth, man, the world itself, yet love grows close. Prepare your flesh as contractors disturb the horizon...all things must pass into sleep or oblivion.

I hear whispers of a communion, beyond privilege, masters, under the moving sky and its intense vastness...Our love grows closer as the flesh turns to the wind and the evening passes, standing above the Earth. She is drunk, diseased, full of artistry and summer roses looking out at the vacant sea. The image doesn't linger just like constellations slowly drifting away from us into the holy dark. Off in the distance, a house...Elysium.

Deciphered and dazzled, the dead live below us in deep dispossession, laughing at our errors and the masks we wear, but the seasons escape them. Rain of time, stranger and companion, prepares us fallen explorers to need our Master. Mentally restored, we burn in our beds, weeping without fear— staring into those late eyes. We grow old, grasping the hands of children. Violence, mask your decency...

*

Carrying the Water

Within the Urn of the Womb the water was carried, heavy and uncertain, until beneath a sky of falling snow the time came. I've heard about that night many times over the decades that once sparkled but seem hazy now. As I look across the old desk at the faded picture of the two of us, it's hard to imagine my life without her. Why? Perhaps because she is my life blood as I'm her flesh and blood. She is my Mother. The Archetype. The Nurturer. The Enigma.

It is said somewhere that as we grow older we begin to see our parents for the first time as ordinary people and not as supposed mythical beings we remember from youth. That is true. If memory is imperfect, our memories of our parents must be imperfect as well. In spite of this, my mother is a constant. That voice on the other end of the telephone reassuring me, or laughing with me, or annoying me. All of it is valuable, and most of it will one day be forgotten too. Not due to wanting its inevitable disappearance, but by the sheer vastness of reality infringing on the mind. Love, however, never fades and etches itself across time as another saying goes.

Which brings me ever closer to the great fortune that befell me on the eighth day of the second month in the year two thousand and eleven...And sometimes memory is perfect, almost too perfect, and all the harshness and hardness that came before him made my resurrection so tangible, forever tangible, as I held him for the first time at 1:20 pm under overcast skies. Yes, the world is forever altered, and yes you feel completely vulnerable so soon after feeling invincible for the first time. That is the miracle of life...The tragedy is not everyone gets to experience its joy.

The smallest, best part of me may one day touch the stars. From womb to womb to better days.

*

Diaries (2)

October 22, 19— ?

The city lies quiet, enmeshed in smoke and fog as though a series of magicians were willing it to disappear. Stepping out from the Old Library with an armful of books, I have a thought there is nothing more the night can offer me other than far away voices and shuttered windows, dead ends, or worse, nothing at all. As I walk through the Western Quarter— normally abuzz with lively music, conversation, and the occasional smell of opium and hashish— it seems subdued, almost sunk in a thick silence even the dead would be envious of in the end. Only a single window above an herbalist shop between two empty bars shines with a heavy crimson glow.

October 1st, 20— ?

What does it mean to truly love someone? Since there are so many different forms of love, how does a person distinguish what kind of love they are feeling for another human being? Therein lies my dilemma...

Unknown date, unknown year

...After a lot of indecision, fall came early. Outside one could only see the border of the fading light. In the city they all watched as the rain fell, creating shallow pools that reflected what little solar energy remained. What do you seek tired traveller? What are you after? The wealth we were promised became our prison; the rest we hoped for became a dream. After years of contemplation our minds gave out, bereft of strength, wisdom, and joy...

Throughout time, or at least my time, there has been a discrepancy between what I think is real or simply imaginary. In one instance everything seems more real than real, yet in the next instance you realize that it was nothing more than a mirage in a vast desert. There are times when one's thoughts drift toward emptiness, for when things seem too good to be true retreating into the void is a safety net. Intuition is an ally and enemy when it comes to uncovering the truth about reality. It plays tricks on you, but it can also supply you with a sense of wonder and hope. So what am I really talking about? I'm talking about affairs of the heart, where intuition is neither your ally nor your enemy...That is where the discrepancies come in, and that is where hope and wonder can flourish.

November 9th, 19— ?

I've been waiting— one could almost say hibernating-- in anticipation for the Process to begin. All people experience the process, but few are conscious of it, and many more never see it to completion. Now the situation has changed so to speak. The door has been opened and our prisoner has been released. God help him.

"It is said we are born from a quiet sleep and at death we slip into a calm awakening."

*

Sator, Arepo, Tenet, Opera, Rotas

From Book Three, Chapter One, of *The Abramelin*

"To know all of things Past and Future, which be not however directly opposed to God, and to his most Holy Will."

Key points: Things past and forgotten. Tribulations to come. To know true and false Friends.

The very nature of writing is both saviour and destroyer, healer and plague. If I accept this to be true, then yes, I have given my life to my past and animated the forgotten out of my dull, grey matter. The tribulation to come is the completion of the Great Work, and through my scribbling I've come to know my true and false friends. It is also through writing I've achieved the dream of Baudrillard: *the perfect crime would be the elimination of the real world.* Extended, the perfect crime would be *the elimination of oneself and forging a new one from the ashes of the old...*

Wind chimes echo across the empty lot, just as the remaining twilight dwindles and the heavy mask of another humid night approaches. Nobody but me on the empty streets. I've been looking for a little bit of something, but I don't know what...I'm sure I'll know when I find it, thinking of...nothing.

*

Corpse of the Butterfly

"There are no endings, just a continuous line that is the trail of infinity," a friend once told me. *"We arrive and depart, yet the essence of who and what we are continues forever, finding its way into the nooks and crannies of the world."* A part of me still held onto the notion that all my failures up to then had done nothing to transform me, but when my friend J. said what he did, my vision began to clear... or so I believed. We stood by the railing on the High Gate Bridge, admiring the river below. J. turned to me, his eyes covered by cheap sunglasses, smiling weakly before continuing...*"A saying attributed to the Buddha says that all the good and evil done in the world since the start of this world is still being felt today...So everything we put out truly effects everything tomorrow."*

I say nothing, thinking instead I would be better off
floating in the cold water.

*

Poissons de Mer

They are called by many names: the Coalition, the
Buzzkills, everything in-between. They are elusive,
mysterious, lost in the rains of the west coast. But out of
all of them stands the one who matters the most: The
Jeweller. In the great cycle that we don't understand,
and the million synchronicities going on in the Great
Expanse, our lives are intertwined. A most unusual twist
in the fabric of space-time. As important as that is, the
Jeweller himself is more important in the story.

We used to possess the night; those quiet and serene
nights sitting on benches drinking narcotic blends or
watching electrical storms between puffs of evergreen.
Weather never hampered us, or the threat of the
Thought Police. We traversed the Four Districts, drank
beer or coffee in darkened cafes...Yes, we were spectres
of the night. And then there are the dreams and
nightmares we inhabited together, where I thought I'd
lost him amongst throngs of people in sinister cities,

amongst gargantuan waves at sea, by sword or gun. A sign, perhaps, that time is limited even in the dream world. He is a man of such amazing talent nothing can truly stop him, for he can dismantle anything with his skilled fingers.

He said once in some papers he left me: *"We are all explorers. Released from the same mysterious abyss to crawl then walk then crawl in this place, this system. From birth to death adrift in an underlying scheme of an order. Despite the chaos, despite the conformity to live and find our place in the bell curve of society."* Well said, Jeweller. One of my mantras.

My mind buzzed as I made my way into the Dragon Court wondering if he had arrived before me. The small park, tucked away behind a small spice market, had the look of a swirling galaxy with many dimmed lights. He stood under the light that flickered the most...

"What's in the envelope? Or is that too forward a question?" I said with a smile.

"You don't want to spoil our conversation piece, do you?" he said with a smirk.

"I can wait; I'm a patient man."

A vortex awaited.

*

Anaïs Nin

The name itself holds a kind of mystery, don't you think? I wish there was enough shelf space to hold every volume of her immense diary, but the one volume I do have and treasure— along with her unique *Cities of the Interior,* and *Delta of Venus*— is her truest statement, as any diary worth its salt should be. In the chronology of her life we see the unravelling of her romance with writer Henry Miller, that "perverted" man who gave the world *Tropic of Cancer* and *Black Spring.* I think I like the latter a little more than the former simply because it's dedicated to her. Reading her work when I did, in my early twenties, gave validation to my feelings and thoughts in a way most people couldn't give me. My emotions were far too raw then, unfocused, and every little thing hurt. Sadly, a lot of that acute sensitivity has fallen by the wayside. I'll say it again if I haven't said so already: *literature saved my life,* and there certainly were times when her words helped me through grim times.

"*I have an emotional tapeworm. Never enough to eat.*"

Sentences like that reminded me we only come close to viewing ourselves properly when we try to write about ourselves, even though we only get a small piece of the picture. Our friends, and especially our enemies, view us much better. What amazes me now about Anaïs Nin is how completely she took the time to observe human relationships and love, and that these things we often take for granted are so often shrouded in greyness the more we examine them with a fine-tooth comb.

Her writing can often be heart-wrenching, and as time goes on I find it more difficult to go back to her words, even though I love them very much. It's the same feeling one has when breaking off a long relationship: you may still love that person but it's impossible to return. The same can be said of my kinship with Anaïs...A prolonged separation. I can only recall recommending her once, perhaps a bit presumptuously because I don't believe most readers would appreciate her prose. Not due to a lack of intelligence, but a lack of emotional and intuitive intelligence. Maybe this is why I don't hear her name mentioned very often, and I find that fact disappointing. One thing is certain: Anaïs and I are hopeless romantics at heart, hoping those high demands we make of ourselves can one day be seen in someone else for us. All or nothing. Love or darkness.

*

Outer Space

The Land which I walk upon is scary...no, terrifying, but the oceans are more terrifying, for in those depths are great unknowns. But when one looks to the Heavens punctuated with ever dying stars, the terrifying aspects accentuate themselves. Amidst the beauty and sadness of Saturn's rings or swirling nebula, the Universe is cold, noiseless, indifferent. This never stopped me from loving its charms and its curves, its radiant strands of light, cosmic dust, floating rocks, and ever-present gravity holding it all together. The Grand Design, whether guided by an invisible hand or random event is hardly the point: diversity is perhaps what matters the most in the End.

Dreams of a Big Crunch go hand in hand with the idea that time will reverse, and all those events dished out by the wispy cosmos swirling about will somehow be put back in the pocket of eternal dark matter. One also imagines deep currents of liquid methane, ancient probes, red skies and alien flowers...

Imagine the thousand lifetimes to a distant star, or how the tail of a comet or meteor falling from skies above came from unseen places untouched by human hands, from depths we will never see. We think of ourselves on our blue-green world as explorers, but really we've made it far enough to see where we come from. We've gone nowhere, so why be so arrogant? We should be humble in the face of infinity... Shouldn't we?

*

Magick

A definition in not so many words, though words themselves hold magical power. Words can change perspective, change the course of history, and perhaps even change *reality* as we see it through the lens of an imperfect eye...129*, 8*, 179*. Not only do words carry power, but numbers do as well. Numbers, like words, become very personal to the individual. These three numbers are mine. Through the lengthy process of synchronicity, various readings, dreams, strange sightings, and deep reflective experiences, I've come to no definitive conclusion about the Universe, except that the only constant is change and the one theory labelled *truth* today becomes tomorrow's falsehood. Nature as we know it seems to be built on a symmetry we have only the smallest conception of, but we still possess the tenacity to use terms such as *faith*. I, too, am guilty of this crime, but only insofar as I deny *reasonable explanations*. Our utmost attachment to *reason* and *empirical evidence* does nothing to help our civilization progress. Only by *experiment of all kinds* and living on the fringes of reason and faith might we see different horizons, eh?

*

Letter 12 (Book)

To my publisher, or would-be publisher: my book is now complete. Many speculated for years if the manuscript in question existed, and I managed to keep the content a secret this whole time, not to mention the *intricate details* that went into composing my magnum opus in a time that seems, at least from my point of view, unequipped or uninterested in diving head first into a sea of reference and info pertaining to obscure people, places, and objects.

*

Knights and Hexagrams

The monsters have grown silent, and the veil of night—
which normally wrapped itself so gently around my
head— has given way to the luminous stars of the
heavens. I walk alone now through the city, open as a
book on its last chapter, only I'm not certain as to how
long or short that chapter will be. Time, as they say, will
tell. The way by which I reached this moment is like
something out of a dream or a dark fantasy, yet as the
days have turned to months, and the months inevitably
into years, I've felt like I've achieved something
monumental, or at least something rare and
undefinable. Truly, I've become someone else
entirely...Sixty-four, sixty-four, one, one twenty-nine.

A Checklist of JEF Titles

* Winners of the Kenneth Patchen Award for the Innovative Novel

Offbeat / Quirky